Two Lies and A Lord

Two Lies and A Lord

ELOISA JAMES

Table of Contents

Episode 90:
Ladies-and Ladybirds

April 18, 1816
Lord Rothingale's Masquerade
London

The Right Honorable Lord Devin—who thought of himself as Miles, though only his sisters addressed him as such—strolled into Lord Rothingale's masquerade planning to stay for ten minutes. At most, fifteen.

Earlier in the day, at their club, his old friend had announced that the most beautiful ladies in London would attend, although his wink promised lady*birds*. Sure enough, courtesans were swarming the ballroom, eagerly looking for their next benefactor.

Miles didn't have a mistress.

He didn't want one.

He felt like that absurd Shakespeare character who moaned about losing his mirth. The lines had been drilled into him at Eton, so they jumped into his head, willy-nilly: *I have of late, (but wherefore I know not) lost all my mirth.*

Oh Christ, he was quoting Hamlet, the ultimate dreary prince. That had to be a sign of mental deterioration.

Hamlet's malaise had dramatic origins—father murdered, mother remarried, etc.—but Miles's complaint was mundane. He was lonely.

Mirth had gone out the window a couple of years ago, after his best friend Jonah fell in love and moved to Suffolk with his wife.

Not that Miles begrudged Jonah the lovely Bea, but he missed his friendship. And damn it, he was jealous. Jonah and Bea didn't coo at each other like doves; they squabbled just as often as they laughed. Yet their bond was so deep that they were happier together than apart.

These days Miles spent most of his time in the House of Lords, serving as the head investigator for charges of murder and depravity amongst the aristocracy. Filling the hours didn't help his malaise, likely because the cases were so beastly—and the criminals seldom punished. The House reeked of inequitable treatment and double standards. He found it hard to shake off the stench after talking to a boot boy beaten to the point of death for the sin of an unpolished shoe, knowing that his master would almost certainly walk free.

Years ago, he would have relished the seductive impropriety of this masquerade, but no longer. He skirted an over-rouged ladybird whose mask did little to conceal her avaricious eyes. Glancing at a couple leaning against the wall, the man's hips pumping rhythmically, he felt only distaste for such vulgarity.

So far he had resisted his family's insistence that he find a wife, but it seemed the time had finally arrived. He was almost thirty, and this Season he'd have nothing else to do while roaming between society events, given that his sister Clementine was already betrothed, and his two younger sisters wouldn't debut until next year.

Obviously, Lord Rothingale's house was no place to find a respectable woman to marry. Hell, the man had tried to entice Clementine into eloping with him, and if Miles hadn't known Rothingale all his life, he wouldn't have darkened his door. But the man was a nobleman, if a degenerate one, and paying respect to those of rank by attending their various events was a gentlemanly pastime, regardless of the host's reputation.

He was turning to leave when his eye was caught by a tumble of white-blonde hair, almost silver under candlelight. The woman in question wore a mask topped by a masquerade hat ringed in violets, her face concealed by the veil that ended just above her plump lips.

She was peering about as if she had lost someone—presumably not the young lout standing beside her, trying to get her attention.

It occurred to Miles that he might have been too hasty in dismissing the idea of a mistress. Or if not that, a mutually enjoyable evening.

Acting from pure instinct, he strode directly to her and smiled. "Good evening."

She tilted her head and blinked at him from behind her veil.

Miles's whole being stilled. He knew those lips.

He had met this lady at her debut ball. He had danced with her, talked to her, eaten with her—before she was exiled from polite society due to her upcoming uncle's trial for treason.

Anger surged in his veins. What in the hell was Miss Daisy Wharton doing at one of the most disreputable parties in all London? He had judged her something of a nitwit with a penchant for mischief—albeit a strikingly beautiful one.

But this was more than mischief.

If anyone recognized her in this den of iniquity, she would be exiled from polite society forever, no matter the outcome of her uncle's trial.

Moreover, the last thing Captain Sir Tyron needed was for his niece's disgraceful behavior to cause another scandal in the family. The captain was currently imprisoned in the Tower of London; the Lord High Steward had accepted the case for adjudication in the House of Lords, which meant it would soon be handed to Miles to investigate.

The man standing on Daisy's other side said aggressively, "You'll have to wait your turn. I already asked this lady to dance, so I've claimed her. She's mine for the evening."

Miles leveled an icy stare that made the ruffian pale and fall back a step. "She is dancing with me." He caught Daisy by the arm and drew her deep onto the dance floor until a crowd of inebriated dancers blocked her admirer's view.

"Sir!" she protested, pulling back.

"Don't you mean 'my lord'?" Miles asked grimly, snatching her right hand as the strains of a waltz began. Naturally, Rothingale's orchestra was playing the scandalous new dance that required a man to hold a woman in his embrace. "You know perfectly well who I am, Miss Wharton." He placed his left hand on her back and began dancing, hoping that no one would notice them in the mass of people.

She gracefully matched his steps, for all she was scowling at him from behind her mask. "Anyone could recognize you, Lord Devin, since you have made no attempt to disguise your identity. You are not wearing a mask, and you're taller than most."

"More to the point, what if someone recognizes *you*? No proper young lady would enter Rothingale's house. The man is a well-known degenerate."

"I was just starting to realize…But how could I have known? My mother received an invitation!"

"Lady Wharton was invited to *this* event? Impossible." He said it flatly because Rothingale would never make a mistake of that nature. The only women invited would be from the *demimonde*, on the fringes of respectable society, if not below.

Her brow pleated. "I suppose it might have been addressed to my father. I didn't notice."

"I suggest that you do not open Lord Wharton's mail in the future."

"'Twas in a pile of invitations!" she protested. "Why would my father receive an invitation to such a disgraceful event? He spends most of his time in the country."

Miles had no intention of answering any questions about Lord Wharton. "Given that you are here without a chaperone, you would be courting scandal even if this were a respectable event. I surmise that you stole out of the house like a schoolboy avoiding chapel."

She didn't answer; she was gazing about with bright curiosity, not looking repentant in the least.

"Surely you don't need me to tell you that your reputation will be ruined if you are recognized here," Miles added in his most autocratic tones, ones that cowed everyone except his sisters.

Rather than burst into tears, she curled her lip. "*You* are here as well, Lord Devin, unmasked and known to all."

"Irrelevant."

"I think not."

"You are an unmarried young lady, and—"

"So no one will want to marry me based on this evening? What of you? You're an unmarried man!"

"The comparison is pointless."

"Granted, you're not precisely an unmarried *young* man!" she retorted. "My presence here is due to a simple mistake. Your presence indicates that you welcome distasteful attachments that have nothing to do with marriage."

Miles prided himself on having an even temperament. When other men raged and stormed, he maintained equanimity. Yet now he found himself so angry that his heart was thumping in his chest. "I'm not yet thirty," he pointed out, avoiding her second point.

"As I said, old!" She tossed her head and more platinum hair spilled down her back. "I suppose you came here hoping to make a ... connection, shall we say?" She turned her head from left to right, her plump lower lip curling as she surveyed the crowd. "I am loath to offend you by questioning your judgement—or your taste."

"I was just leaving."

She raised an eyebrow, so he growled begrudgingly, "No, I do not have a mistress, nor was I looking for one. You are remarkably blunt. I would be greatly offended if my sisters brought up this topic."

"Then you should be comforted by the thought that they probably haven't the knowledge to do so. Ladylike ignorance makes it easier for a gentleman to indulge in extramarital activities without his wife's knowledge."

Daisy said it evenly, without bitterness or sarcasm, but Miles winced inwardly. Even leaving her own familial situation aside, she was right about the inequitable treatment of the sexes. His disagreeable work in the House of Lords had taught him that most ladies were horrified to encounter garden-variety debauchery, let alone more esoteric practices.

He whirled her about just in time to avoid the drunken lurch of a giggling couple. "You waltz very well."

"You also dance well," Daisy replied with the air of someone forced into civility. "Unfortunately, the scandal surrounding my uncle's charge of treason means that I shan't have a chance to waltz again until next Season, after I'm approved by Almack's patronesses."

"If anyone recognizes you here, Almack's will be the least of your problems," Miles said. "As soon as this dance concludes, we will slip away, hopefully without notice."

"I shouldn't have made such a personal remark about your reasons for attending this masquerade," Daisy said suddenly. "I apologize. We genuinely thought the event would be akin to that given annually by the Duchess of—"

Miles interrupted her. "*We?*"

She looked surprised. "My cousin Livie and I."

Of course Daisy wouldn't have snuck out alone. He should have known that Olive Tyron would have accompanied her; they had grown up together and seemed as close as sisters. He took a breath and controlled his temper. "Where is Miss Tyron?"

"Livie is here somewhere," Daisy said, glancing about. "She was just behind me, but a press of people entered with us, and I lost her in the crowd. I was looking for her when you pulled me into this waltz. I think she must have gone right when I went left, so likely she's in that room." She nodded toward an archway.

Miles's temper slipped its leash entirely. "You are a pair of idiots," he said scathingly. "Don't you know that the House of Lords is investigating your uncle's supposed treason—an investigation that I will be running? Believe me when I say that Captain Sir Tyron's case would be negatively impacted by his daughter creating another scandal. He *must* keep the sympathy and loyalty of his fellow aristocrats in order to beat this charge."

Daisy missed a step, her mouth rounding with horror. "I had no idea."

"Not to mention the fact that your cousin might have been accosted by a lecher like the one back there who 'claimed' you for the evening."

She raised her chin. "Livie would never allow herself to be taken advantage of."

"You have no idea what you're talking about. A man could jerk you into his arms and kiss you—or worse—and no one here would bat an eyelash. We must find her immediately."

"Livie can defend herself," Daisy snapped.

Thankfully, the waltz was ending, so Miles wrapped his arm around her waist and drew her to the side of the room.

"You are holding me improperly. I am contemplating whether to kick you sharply in the shins or stick you with a hatpin," Daisy informed him. She pulled a pin from her masquerade hat and waved it proudly.

She was an extraordinary mixture of sophisticated and naïve, old and young. Irritatingly, she fit perfectly in the shelter of his arm. "The next time a man embraces you inappropriately, I suggest that you act rather than air your options."

She rolled her eyes at him. "It's only you."

Miles wasn't sure how to take that. "What is Miss Tyron wearing?" he asked, as they walked through the archway into the other chamber.

Daisy cleared her throat. He glanced down at her.

"My cousin..." Her voice faltered.

"What?"

"She's there...over there on that settee."

Miles looked.

A woman wearing a scarlet domino and a masquerade hat was sitting in a young army officer's lap, her arms wound around his neck, kissing him enthusiastically.

"Bloody hell," he growled.

Daisy looked up at him, eyes wide. "Of the two of us, *I'm* the naughty one."

What he said next was unrepeatable.

Episode 91:
Eleven Months Later

Eleven Months Later
March 1, 1817
Townhouse of Lord and Lady Wharton
London

"We must behave as if we are in half-mourning until Christmas at the earliest," Lady Wharton instructed. "No bouncing around the dancefloor or loud giggling, Daisy. If we display the slightest hint of pleasure, we shall be accused of being unfeeling."

"Yes, Mother," Daisy replied, nodding.

"Tomorrow night, at the Duchess of Trent's opening ball, I will conduct myself soberly, as if garbed in sackcloth and ashes."

Daisy knew perfectly well that her mother planned to wear a magnificent gown of periwinkle-blue satin adorned with a circlet of diamonds; a costume farther from sackcloth could hardly be imagined. She nodded again. "Of course."

Her mother looked at her sharply. "My gown is *dark* blue. Very close to gray. I believe sackcloth is brown, but the color is ruinous for my complexion." Dismissing that sartorial observation, she began leafing through a thick stack of invitations that had arrived in the previous week.

Before her uncle's trial for treason, followed by his death by apoplexy on learning that he was going to be convicted for murder, Daisy would have relished a lively debate on the suitability of diamonds with sackcloth, but these days she tried not to upset her mother's equilibrium. Lady Wharton veered between fretting and brooding, interspersed with frequent bouts of tears.

"Everyone but the haughtiest of sticklers will welcome my daughter back to society," Lady Wharton muttered to herself. "Daisy's dowry and breeding are excellent, and her beauty is incomparable."

Last Season, the thoroughly dislikable Lady Regina had mocked Daisy for being "short, fat, and unkempt," which had stung at the time. Since then, based on ogling males, Daisy had concluded that her plump bosom was an asset in husband-hunting. And Lord Argyle had not labeled her hair unkempt but compared it to a moon's nimbus.

Which he then kindly clarified as a "luminous cloud of moonbeams."

So who cared what Lady Regina thought?

"Livie and I had plenty of suitors last Season before my uncle's circumstances forced us to withdraw," she reminded her mother.

"Your cousin's marriage does clear the field, making you one of the most eligible ladies on the market," her mother said, taking a practical view of the matter. "Unfortunately, Robert de Lacy Evans is now betrothed, and Lord Argyle married over the summer. It's a pity he didn't wait for you." She brightened. "Of course, Livie's brother-in-law, Lord Frederick FitzRoy-Paget, is both unmarried and a future earl."

"Fond though I am of Frederick, he's an inebriate," Daisy noted.

"The Earl of Winchester is looking for a wife after his betrothal to Lady Regina broke down," Lady Wharton added, with a touch of uncertainty.

The man Daisy and Livie had compared to a scallion? Never. "Any man foolish enough to betroth himself to Regina is not someone I'd care to marry."

Lady Wharton snatched a missive out of the pile and broke the seal, her fingers trembling slightly. A ticket fell out. "Thank goodness," she cried. "Lady Castlereigh has reissued your Almack's voucher."

Daisy scowled. "What about Livie's?" Back when her uncle was first accused of treason, Almack's had promptly withdrawn admission vouchers from both girls.

"Livie no longer needs a voucher," her mother said, looking up. "She is happily married and living abroad, as we shall inform anyone impertinent enough to inquire."

"Yes, but—"

"Do not mention his name!" Lady Wharton's voice rose to a pitch. "My brother, my own brother—" She choked, dropping Lady Castlereigh's note back on the table before she rose and walked across the room to the window, wrapping her arms around her waist.

Daisy hopped up and went to her side, giving her a consoling hug and a handkerchief.

Her mother blotted her eyes. "It was bad enough when he was accused of treason! But *murder?* How shall I ever live it down? I dread the thought of walking into a ballroom."

"We must remember that Capt—that *he*—died before he was actually convicted," Daisy offered.

"Pshaw! That poor boy," her mother continued unsteadily. "That poor, poor boy."

While captaining a navy vessel, Daisy's uncle had ordered a young sailor named Jeremy Tulip to be thrown overboard for a minor infraction, and the lad had either been eaten by sharks or drowned.

"Naturally, my brother had no concern about the damage he's done! One of the last things he said to me was that he intended to put the whole unpleasantness out of his mind. That's what he called it: an 'unpleasantness.' Sometimes I just hate men." Lady Wharton's voice crackled with grief.

"I understand," Daisy said, handing over another handkerchief. She had begun carrying three or four.

"My brother may have left this world, but that's not far enough. I would be pleased never to hear his name again. *Ever.* The moment I walk into the Trent ballroom, he is all anyone will speak about. They'll be asking me with feigned sincerity how I feel after my loss. And what am I to say to that? How does the family of a murderer grieve his loss?"

"Not for long," Daisy promised. "The world will quickly move to the next scandal."

Her mother swallowed hard and mopped her eyes again. "I have spent years establishing myself as an ethical, upstanding member of polite society. Merely for a cruel, selfish man to drag my reputation through the mud."

"Livie cannot be blamed for her father's transgressions—and neither can you, for your brother's," Daisy said, for approximately the thousandth time.

Lady Wharton drew in an unsteady breath. "At least the Tulip family will live in comfort from now on."

Daisy nodded. Her mother had forced her unrepentant brother to give the Tulips a large sum of money before he died. "Every family has a black sheep, Mother, and my uncle is ours. After a few months, no one will chatter about the murder, any more than they talk of Lord Byron's *affaire* with his half-sister."

Her mother gasped, and her mouth fell open.

Oops.

Daisy had a tendency to speak—and act—before thinking.

"*Daisy!*" Lady Wharton dropped her handkerchief to the floor and clutched her bosom like an actress at Drury Lane. "I cannot believe my ears! That my own daughter should allow such odious words to cross her lips! I am shocked...scandalized... *disgusted!*"

"I apologize," Daisy said, arranging her features to look as penitent as she could. It wasn't one of her skills; she should probably practice that expression before the mirror. She could employ it when people asked about her uncle.

"How do you even know of that blackguard, let alone his brazen-faced sister? Who would tell an innocent young lady about such a disgusting a personage as Lord Byron?"

Daisy sighed. "Everyone knows. Miss Augusta Leigh bore him a daughter, after all."

"But you are a young, untouched, innocent—"

"My point is that scandals come and go," Daisy said, before her mother could start thinking too hard about her supposed innocence.

She wasn't dissolute, though she knew more about the world than Lady Wharton would imagine. Most young ladies hadn't read a useful book called *City of Eros*, for example.

Daisy had read it twice.

"If you are tarred with the brush of hedony," her mother gasped, getting up a new head of steam, "if society decides that you are a debauched coquette, that will be the end of this family. *The end!* I shall live out my final days in sackcloth in a darkened room! *Brown* sackcloth!"

"I don't think 'hedony' is a word," Daisy observed.

"Stop smirking and listen to me! This family's reputation will recover far faster from my brother's misconduct than it would from a scandal of yours along the lines of Lord Byron's."

"That's so unfair. Murder is far more indicative of a corrupt soul than wanton behavior."

"Not in the civilized world," Lady Wharton declared. "If a woman is not chaste, she is *nothing*. If the subject ever rises again, you must pretend that you have no idea how babies are made." She narrowed her eyes. "Which I gather you do. Somehow. I have certainly never mentioned the subject."

"It's absurd that women have to pretend to be ignorant of basic facts about their own physiology," Daisy said, beginning to feel heated. "What's more, everyone knows that gentlemen have fancies outside marriage. Of course, it would have been far better of Byron to seduce someone other than his half-sister—"

"*Daisy!*"

"It was terrible, most improper," Daisy added hastily. "He is a dissolute rake—"

"Never let his name pass your lips again!" her mother cried wildly.

"But a good poet," Daisy finished.

"The verse of an incestuous devil!" Lady Wharton gasped. "Surely you have not read that execrable nonsense."

Daisy wouldn't say that she had a penchant for fibbing, but quite often one had to find one's way *around* the truth. For example, Captain Sir Tyron wouldn't allow his daughter to read anything but the most "deserving" texts, so Daisy had read many books aloud when her cousin Livie happened to be in the room.

City of Eros, for example.

And Byron's *Fugitive Pieces*, which had been remarkably instructive, as when Byron vowed to enter his lady's chamber and "love for hours together."

Obviously, she and Livie had needed to understand what "love" meant when used as a verb in the context of a bedroom. Their maid, Ada, had been most enlightening.

"I don't believe most of Byron's works are in print," Daisy said now, dodging the question.

"You must never read them," her mother demanded, her eyes bulging slightly. "This family stands on the very edge, the precipice of ruin, and your behavior must be impeccable. Tomorrow, you will look like a subdued angel, your eyes cast to the floor, modesty and remorse on full display."

Daisy couldn't stop herself. "To be honest, Mother, I'll look more like an Egyptian mummy than an angel."

"Fiddlesticks!"

"Remember all those lengths of white satin? I had my final fitting yesterday."

Her opening gown for the Season had been designed with panels of silk falling from a high waist, intended to lightly float around the wearer's body. But Lady Wharton had ordered the *modiste* to use a heavier fabric and add three times as many panels as in the original design.

If Lady Regina thought Daisy was fat last year, wait til the lady caught sight of her in this gown.

"Nonsense!" Lady Wharton snapped. "The dress is fashionable and appropriate. Your hair will stay in a chignon, or I'll fire your maid. No lip color, of course. A *jeune fille*, but without French sauciness."

Daisy nodded. She could do it.

And she *would* have done it too ...

If the entire back of her gown hadn't ripped clear off her body.

On the dancefloor.

Episode 92:
The Jesters' Corner

March 2, 1817
The Duchess of Trent's ball
The opening event of the 1817 Season

Naturally, having made up his mind to spend the Season looking for a wife, Miles no sooner entered the Trent ballroom than he caught sight of a lady who was manifestly ineligible for that honor.

With ten months' further acquaintance with Daisy Wharton, he was no longer surprised by the fact she had attended the Rothingale masquerade. Although he had dragged her out of that house, she had spent her time since merrily engaging in impudent mischief, such as smuggling a file to her uncle in the Tower of London.

Admittedly, she had been instrumental in proving that same uncle's innocence of the charge of treason.

As for the charge of murder? No one could clear Tyron's name from that accusation, even though his solicitor had done an excellent job of painting Jeremy Tulip as a ne'er-do-well, while prosing on about Sir Tyron's medal for bravery in the French wars.

And now, of course, Daisy Wharton had returned to polite society. She was standing beside her mother, the swirl of hair atop her head precariously held in place by diamond-clad butterflies. Her gown covered her like a shroud, but even so she was ... exquisite.

With a start, he looked away, surveying a ballroom full of ladies with pale lips and orderly hair.

Daisy was far too young and foolish to consider as a wife. Perhaps she wasn't overly young, but foolish? In the extreme. Impulsive and reckless. She courted scandal: just look at the way she and her cousin used to gallop at top speed through Hyde Park, something no proper lady would do.

In fact, now that he thought of it, Daisy might still be galloping in the park, even though her cousin had married and moved abroad. He should impress upon her the undesirability of that behavior.

It took him two hours to make his way to her side, thanks to his sister Clementine having spread the news that he intended to find a wife. One young woman actually stabbed him with her fan to gain his attention.

When Miles finally reached Daisy, she had just finished dancing with the future Earl Paget. Frederick wasn't entirely drunk, nor entirely sober.

About the same as always, in other words.

Miles bowed. "Good evening, Miss Wharton. Lord FitzRoy-Paget."

Daisy's face stilled, and her smile fell away as she curtsied. "Lord Devin. How do you do?"

"Evening, Devin," Frederick said, more genially. "How's the pursuit of murderers serving you these days?"

"I don't pursue murderers," Miles replied. "I investigate criminal charges when Earl Paget—your father—requests my assistance. Miss Wharton, it is a pleasure."

"We could help you," Frederick offered. "As we did last time, deciphering those coded letters. Daisy and I made an excellent pair of investigators, don't you think? If we hadn't been born to the wrong families, we could have become Bow Street Runners."

Daisy's eyes began dancing. "*You* could have become a Runner," she pointed out. "*I* was born to the wrong gender."

"I have no need for assistance," Miles told them.

"I doubt that," Frederick drawled. "You were sending people all over France looking for that traitor, remember? Any fool could have told you that the man had to be a Londoner."

"Actually, Frederick," Daisy said, "*I* made that point, and I do not consider myself a 'fool.'"

Miles had the distinct feeling that she considered him to be the fool in question. "Miss Wharton, may I have the honor of a dance?" he asked, rather coldly.

Daisy flipped open her fan and looked at its bare spines as if she were hoping a few signatures had miraculously appeared. "As you can see, you may have whichever dance you choose," she responded, without visible enthusiasm.

"I'll take you in for supper," Frederick promised. "Daisy isn't enjoying the same popularity as last Season," he told Miles. "I suspect the murderous uncle has put them off. Likely the young fools are afraid that she'll put arsenic in their tea if they put a step wrong."

Daisy snapped her fan shut and tapped her lips, drawing attention to her mouth. Her lips were the deep ruby of port wine, but Miles could have sworn that she wore no lip color. Her eyelashes were darker than her hair, though she hadn't turned them sooty with coal; they fringed her blue eyes like—

He tore his mind out of an absurd riot of similes. He didn't care about the color of her eyes.

"A woman should plan for her future," Daisy said. "What missteps should I consider worthy of arsenic? After all, my uncle has set a standard for criminality that might be hard to match."

"Adultery," Frederick said promptly.

Perhaps Lord Fitzroy-Paget thought she would turn pink at the word, or hide behind her fan, or giggle madly. Miles knew better.

"Adultery is so common that avenging it might be taken amiss," Daisy retorted, not flicking an eyelash. "Like killing a husband because he slurps his tea, which frankly, might actually tempt me to homicide."

Frederick burst out laughing, but Miles just raised an eyebrow. The man who'd stray from Miss Daisy Wharton's bed? He didn't exist.

"Oh dear, I've shocked you," Daisy said to Miles. She flicked open her fan and hid behind it. "Give me a minute..."

When she dropped her fan, her whole face had changed. Her eyes were now soft and bewildered, her lower lip trembling. "I protest and vow, Lord FitzRoy-Paget, that you have shocked me to the bone. 'Tis a horrendous shock to hear such a nasty word spoken in my presence. I must beg you to have more care for my innocence."

"Impressive," Miles said, unable to hold back a smile.

"Yes, especially because a young lady would have to know the meaning of adultery in order to *be* offended," Daisy pointed out. "Ignorance and innocence are not always synonymous."

"Moving on," Frederick said. "Let's pretend you transform yourself into an avenging angel for the chaste wives of London, Daisy. If you poisoned every faithless man in this city, there'd scarcely be an intact marriage left."

"So I have assumed, Frederick. So I have assumed." Daisy flicked a glance at Miles from under her lush eyelashes, her expression suggesting that she had not forgotten Miles's appearance at the Rothingale masquerade.

Miles used to think her a nitwit, but after she helped crack the code of a traitor's letters, he'd come to the conclusion that she was one of the most intelligent women he knew.

Albeit mischievous, impulsive, and prone to telling falsehoods.

"Personally, I believe that murder is worse than adultery," Frederick said thoughtfully. "It is unfortunate that society will forgive the first, but not the second. Your uncle is a case in point. I shouldn't have been shocked when the House of Lords acquitted him, but I was." He took a swig of whiskey.

"Stop drinking," Daisy said, poking him in the side. "I promised Livie that I'd do my part to rehabilitate your reputation and your liver."

"Daisy plans to shove me on the market...if she doesn't marry me herself," Frederick told Miles.

"You've set yourself a challenge, Miss Wharton," Miles remarked.

"That's an insult...Pistols at dawn!" Frederick shouted giddily, collecting glances from a good half of the ballroom—who instantly looked away when they saw who had bellowed, their mouths screwed up with disapproval.

Somewhat surprisingly, Miles discovered he was scowling back at them. Frederick might not be a perfect gentleman—obviously he drank too much—but he was far cleverer than most in the room.

Further, there was something wounded behind his mocking eyes. He was an impudent, careless jester, but more interesting than most of the pompous lords Miles dealt with in the House, many of whom had readily excused Sir Tyron for throwing a boy to the sharks.

Daisy was smiling at Frederick as if she...

People might misinterpret their friendship based on her expression. He'd seen it happen; his friend Jonah had been obligated to marry after he was compromised.

No, that wasn't true. Jonah married because he was desperately in love with Bea. Daisy couldn't possibly feel that for Frederick.

"I know you formed a friendship during the last year, but you shouldn't address each other by your given names in public," he said before he thought better. "It might be misunderstood."

Frederick elbowed Daisy. "Lord Devin is worried for your reputation. Isn't that sweet of him? Don't worry. I'll marry you no matter how scandalous you become. I intend to limit my prospects to wallflowers anyway, so my spouse and I can huddle together and gossip."

"You plan to form a jester's corner with your wife?" Miles asked. Oddly, it sounded... rather fun. More enjoyable than pacing around the dance floor discussing the habitats of snowy owls, as he had done earlier in the evening when Miss Appleton treated him to a lecture.

"What's a jester's corner?" Daisy asked.

"You do know that British kings had official jesters?"

She nodded.

"When a jester wasn't actively mocking the crown, he retreated to the corner of the throne room and mocked society at large," Miles explained.

"That would suit me," Frederick said. "I need to find a wife who doesn't mind wearing a cap with bells. Perhaps if I adorned the cap with diamonds I could entice someone to my corner. Daisy?"

"Even given that suitors are thin on the ground, I have to refuse your proposal," she said. "A jester's hat would never fit over my hair."

"You do seem to have an outsized pile on your head," Frederick commented. "I'll introduce you to a few of my pals. You'll have more tipsy men at your feet than you can count."

"Miss Wharton doesn't wish to marry an inebriate," Miles growled.

"I don't have any particular dislike of drunks," Daisy said. "One wants one's husband to be occupied, and cheroots have such a terrible odor. Drinking is better than smoking."

"I already have an occupation as court jester," Frederick pointed out.

"I suppose 'old maid' will be mine," Daisy said cheerfully.

She was the farthest thing from an old maid that Miles had ever seen. If she didn't have suitors, it was because they hadn't yet met her. Heard her laughter. *Seen* her laughing.

Even her chortle was sensual. When her lips curled, when she teased, he felt it in every part of his body—some places more than others.

A gentleman didn't *marry* a woman he wanted to throw up against a wall. You'd have to be mad to court a woman who joked about adultery, who was obviously brimming with passion.

"Both of my suitors are kindness personified," Daisy said, smiling at the two of them.

Before he caught himself, Miles choked. True, he had stood talking to her for longer than he had any other woman, but...

Daisy burst into a throaty laugh. "I misspoke! I gather, Lord Devin, that you're no suitor of mine."

Frederick squinted at him. "Revealed your terror, did you? Not very flattering, old chap. You have to learn to disguise your expressions. You looked ready to expire from boredom while dancing with Miss Appleton. You'll never find a wife that way."

Miles cleared his throat. "I would be honored to marry Miss Wharton. Of course."

Thankfully, Daisy showed no signs of being insulted. "It was a reasonable assumption on my part—you *did* ask me to dance—but not to worry. I shan't hold you to it."

"Every man who asks you to dance is not a suitor," Frederick pointed out. "The royal dukes, for example. Certain to ask, given your bosom, but unavailable for marriage."

Daisy patted Miles on the arm. "Only desperate women like me engage in such sad arithmetic. You are free to court where you will."

Horrifyingly, that light touch sent a stunning feeling down his arm, like a burn. Burns are *bad*, he informed his unruly body, which seemed determined to move closer to the fire.

"You do have two suitors, since you also have Jeremiah Hemlock at your beck and call," Frederick said. "Do you know him, Devin?"

"I vaguely remember the name ... but no," Miles said. Of course he wasn't wooing Daisy. On the other hand, he didn't like thinking of other men doing so, and he'd be damned if she married Frederick.

"One of the Arch Rogues, so-called. Supposedly, he's pledged to find a wife in order to win a bet, an unwholesome reason. Plus he has a reputation as a ne'er-do-well. No dancing *or* following him into the shrubbery," Frederick said to Daisy, sounding like a hectoring older brother.

"I can't afford to refuse to dance with one of the few men who's requested my hand," Daisy said, sounding like an irritated little sister.

Of course, Miles *could* introduce her to eligible gentlemen.

But for some reason ... he didn't want to.

Episode 93:
The Pillar of Salt

"If your gown didn't graze your collarbone, you'd have flocks of men around you," Frederick said, pulling the flask from his pocket again. "Wait until they see you in a garment that flatters your curves rather than swaddles them."

Daisy wrinkled her nose. "I told my mother that I look like an Egyptian mummy."

Lord Devin didn't glance at her, of course. He was the most proper man she'd ever met. Other men ogled her body, especially her breasts, but his attention never dipped below her chin. It brought out all her worst tendencies. She wanted to *make* him look.

Which was absurd.

She couldn't imagine why he was standing around talking to her and Frederick.

People might assume he was courting her, which he would obviously loathe. Though she'd masked it with a smile, the shocked look on his face when she referred to him as a suitor was one of the more humiliating moments in her life, right up there with Lady Regina calling her fat.

Unfortunately, Lord Devin always chanced across her at the worst moments, as at the Rothingale masquerade, which had been—she could admit it—a huge mistake. Her mother would have had an apoplexy if she had discovered that Daisy and her cousin had crept out of the house to attend such a sordid event.

As a matter of conscience, Daisy had made up her mind to stop courting scandal. No more rebellion. Lady Wharton's heart couldn't take it; she was already suffering from palpitations multiple times a day.

Unlike Lord Devin, Frederick readily eyed her up and down. "You resemble a pillar of salt. A biblical look but not enticing, if you'll forgive the slur."

"I'm not a scholar," Daisy said. "What's a pillar of salt?"

"Surely you've heard the story," Frederick answered, taking a hearty swig of whiskey. "I was under the impression that ladies regularly flaunt their virtue by warming the pews."

For a moment Daisy thought of fibbing. Yet did she really care what Lord Devin thought of her? Some secret part of her insisted that she did, but she crushed it and chose the truth.

"I fancy you won't be terribly surprised to learn that I prefer to stay at home on the couch reading a novel with no improving content," she replied.

"'Twas the fate of Lot's wife," Lord Devin said. "She and her husband were fleeing the wicked cities of Sodom and Gomorrah. Angels had told her not to look back, but she did, so she was turned to a pillar of salt for her disobedience."

"Oh, now I remember the story," Daisy said unenthusiastically. "Mrs. Lot's skirts were probably dragging in the sand, so she turned back to give them a shake. She was reduced to a pile of salt as punishment for a fallen hem."

"If you don't mind a sartorial suggestion," Frederick said, "*your* skirts are dragging on the floor. I almost tripped over them during that Polonaise."

Daisy twitched her gown away from his feet. "That would be because you missed the steps so often."

Frederick shrugged.

"My mother does not care for the current fashion of skirts that float above the ankles," she added.

To her horror, Lady Regina suddenly appeared at Frederick's side. The lady was—of course—dripping with diamonds, as well as being slim and tall, her hair true gold, which perfectly set off eyes as blue as a lake.

One of those arctic lakes, the ones that are icy year-round.

"Good evening!" she cried. "I feel that societal standards have grown too, too rigid, so I am eager to greet Miss Wharton, as her...unconventional perspective is newly returned to us." She dropped a shallow curtsy.

Very Regina-esque: a greeting accompanied by a reminder of family disgrace.

Daisy forced herself to smile as she curtsied in return.

Regina bared all her teeth while greeting Lord Devin, which was interesting. She had lost her fiancé last Season after making a play for Frederick's brother, throwing herself into Major FitzRoy's arms and kissing him, and thereafter claiming to be betrothed. Unfortunately for her, the major promptly married Livie, propriety be damned.

Lord Devin was more gentlemanly: if Regina threw herself at him, he would be trapped. Never mind the rumors about his rakehellish youth; these days his lordship was every inch an honorable gentleman. Except when he was attending Rothingale's parties, of course.

"You were discussing Miss Wharton's skirts when I joined you, were you not?" Regina asked.

"Actually, we were engaged in biblical exegesis," Frederick drawled.

Regina ignored him. "Miss Wharton and I are wearing the same fashion." Her hand fluttered next to her narrow waist, drawing everyone's attention to the panels of shell-pink silk floating over her rose underskirt. When she danced, the cloth would drift in the breeze, giving a glimpse of her slender thighs. Her skirts were short enough that anyone could see her ankles without waiting for her hem to lift.

If Frederick and Lord Devin were supposed to bubble over with compliments, Regina had chosen the wrong audience. They both looked bored.

"Your gown is lovely," Daisy said, because her mother had brought her up with manners.

"Yours is...interesting," Regina replied, because apparently her mother hadn't bothered. "A panel gown is better fashioned in silk. Satin is so heavy, wouldn't you agree?"

"Lady Wharton was most anxious that my figure not be overly exposed." It was a triumph *not* to glance at Regina's bony legs, outlined in her light gown. That would be unkind.

"I understand," Regina said.

Daisy blinked at her, surprised by the unexpected sympathy in her tone. Regina sounded genuinely warm.

She flipped open her fan and whispered. "It must be so challenging to disguise your extra bulk. I have defects that I must hide as well. My dressmaker told me that my knees are a liability. A *liability!*"

"I'm sorry to hear that," Daisy managed.

Regina dropped her fan and fluttered her eyelashes. "Lord Devin, I was so pleased to see that you have torn yourself away from all that *terribly* important work you do in the House of Lords."

His lordship seemed to have woken up to the idea that Regina was viewing him as a possible husband; his expression held precisely the same distaste as when Daisy labeled him her suitor. He really was a swine.

In fact, he deserved Regina.

"Lord Devin is an old friend," Daisy said.

Regina blinked rapidly. "Ah."

"We, that is, his old friends such as Lord FitzRoy-Paget and me—" she elbowed Frederick, who was leaning against the wall staring into space "—are most anxious that his lordship find a wife worthy of his exalted position."

Lord Devin's eyes darkened. He didn't precisely glare at her, but it was something close.

Regina preened and gave Daisy a genuine smile. "I can understand your concern. These days aristocratic blood is being regularly diluted by unions with those from the mercantile classes."

Daisy gave Lord Devin a sunny smile. "I believe the conductor just announced a waltz. Perhaps you might lead Lady Regina into the dance, if she has not already promised it to another gentleman."

"As it happens, I have not," Regina said, curling her gloved hand around her fan so that none of the signatures were legible.

"I promised to escort *you* onto the dancefloor, Miss Wharton," Lord Devin said untruthfully. "It seems you have forgotten, but as a gentleman, I could not take another lady before you."

"Alas, I am not yet approved to waltz," Daisy said.

The spark in his eye told her that he remembered perfectly well the waltz they shared at the Rothingale masquerade—at least until he dragged her off the dancefloor.

"No proper debutante would waltz before one of the patronesses of Almack's approves her for that privilege," Lady Regina said importantly. "I'm afraid that the lapse in Miss Wharton's membership in Almack's might—through no fault of her own—make them hesitant to extend that honor. Such a pity."

Daisy let her eyes mock Lord Devin because ... why not? "I'm afraid I'll have to decline. Such a pity, as Lady Regina says."

His eyes smoldered at her, for all the world like a stage villain. Oh dear, his lordship was annoyed. Daisy kept her expression clear and her eyes innocent.

"I remember when I wasn't free to waltz," Lady Regina chattered, as Lord Devin turned to the side to greet an acquaintance. "Lord FitzRoy-Paget, are you awake?"

Frederick opened his eyes and focused on the lady. "No. Surely only in a nightmare would the woman who tried to compromise my own brother consider it appropriate to converse with me."

Lady Regina drew in her breath sharply. "Your brother ... I shall say no more, as maidenly modesty forbids it!"

"Really?" Frederick looked slightly more awake. "Tell me more about maidenly modesty. I thought it had gone the way of dragons. Magnificent beasts, but nowhere to be found outside legend. My brother—Major FitzRoy—made it sound as if you were St. George and he the dragon to be slain."

Daisy gave Frederick a reproving glance. Society at large had no idea that Regina had made a desperate attempt to compromise Livie's husband, first by kissing him and then by announcing their betrothal. It would be very unkind of Frederick to reveal the truth.

Lady Regina turned to Daisy and laughed shrilly. "His lordship is attempting to be humorous. Major FitzRoy's desire to bring his wife to the battlefields of Europe was sufficient to end our betrothal!"

Daisy didn't like or trust Lady Regina. In fact, she clearly remembered telling her cousin that she planned to squash Regina under her slipper.

But now she had the distinct impression that Regina was anxious. Even lonely. And terrified that people would find out the reason why her latest betrothal came to naught.

"Where are your friends, the Misses Massinger?" Daisy asked, glancing around.

Regina hunched a shoulder. "Petunia married over the summer, and Prudence is hidden in the country because she has conceived again."

In short, her friends had married, and Regina was still trying to find a fiancé who would stay with her, unlike her previous two... or was it three? Granted, Regina had played a part in her broken betrothals, but the major's rejection last Season must have been particularly humiliating.

No trampling of Lady Regina.

At that moment, Lord Devin turned back to their group, drawing forward one of the most powerful women in polite society. "Lady Castlereigh, won't you please allow me to escort Miss Wharton into the next dance? I gather she is not yet approved to waltz."

The lady raised an eyebrow. "How interesting that you have decided to throw your hat into that particular ring," she murmured before raising her voice. "Do waltz with Miss Wharton, Lord Devin. I'm sure your august presence will prove an excellent influence."

"You must be joking," Frederick muttered.

"I shall save you the first waltz after supper," Regina informed Lord Devin. "In fact, we might share the meal to make certain that we locate each other."

"Excellent," the gentleman murmured, bowing.

"I've got a headache," Frederick said to Daisy. "I'll have a lie-down in the library. Come find me if you need me."

He'd pass out on the sofa, but it was better to pry Frederick upright than find herself standing alone or joining her mother in the dowagers' corner. She was lucky to have Frederick as a friend.

Though not, perhaps, as a suitor.

Episode 94:
A Disaster While Dancing

Miles bowed before Daisy and placed his left hand on her back. His fingers tingled, and he found himself wrestling with an inappropriate wave of desire. Daisy may *look* like a pillar of salt, but she smelled like apple blossoms. Up close, her lips were utterly delectable: not port wine but sour cherries. Damn it.

She fit perfectly in his arms, moving fluidly backward as he stepped forward, both of them following the steps with easy skill.

"Are you insulted?" Daisy asked.

Miles shook off the effect of her smile. "Insulted by what?"

"I believe Lady Castlereigh implied that your silvered hair makes you a respectable escort to waltz with me."

"I do not have silvered hair!"

Daisy squinted at his head. "Not yet."

"She implied that you are a minx," he pointed out.

"I suppose I should be insulted, but unlike 'adultery,' I'm not certain of the qualifications for a 'minx.' Do I simply flirt?" Her expression was ...

She was flirting with him.

She probably flirted with everyone. Miles instinctively tried to rein in his body's enthusiastic response to the twinkle in her eye, the twinkle that suggested she found him desirable. The twinkle that made him want to kiss her here, on the dancefloor, which would be insanity.

Still, he instinctively drew her closer, their legs brushing as they moved through the steps of the waltz. Even all those layers of satin couldn't disguise her high, plump breasts, distractingly close to his chest as she leaned into his embrace. "Stop it, minx," he said, his voice dropping to a growl.

Her laughter washed over him like music. They had reached the bottom of the long ballroom, so he turned her in a circle, and then another for the pure delight of it. She swirled with perfect grace, an impudent smile curling the edges of her mouth.

Hunger made him shudder—No, that was disdain, Miles told himself hastily. He couldn't be feeling more than garden-variety lust for a woman as impulsive as Daisy. She was not only impulsive, but reckless.

Right now, that didn't sound like a defect in a wife. In fact, as more strands of moonlit hair fell to her shoulders, marriage seemed like a very good idea, because he could kiss her every time she looked at him with that expression.

No.

She laughed too much to be his wife. Too often.

Often *at him*.

"So, shall we discuss politics?" Daisy asked in an interested voice. "Wait, let's not. I don't know anything about the subject, and I'm not in the mood for a lecture. Have you ever read a novel?"

Miles shook his head. He couldn't think of anything to say other than a blunt and impractical statement: *I want you.* Not as a wife—just because she was the most carnal woman of his acquaintance.

"Now you," she commanded as they made one final turn and headed back up the long ballroom. "Ask me something."

Other women danced like sticks, their backs straight and their limbs rigid. Was it possible to dance and strut at the same time?

He cleared his throat. "How are you faring?"

"Given my lack of suitors, you mean?"

"Actually, I was referring to your uncle's courtroom battle and subsequent demise."

Daisy pursed her lips, sending a wave of lust down Miles's legs. Damn it.

"I'm all right. Careful of my skirts," she added.

As the music drew to a close, he fell back just in time to allow her to sweep the panels that made up her gown to the side. The satin flattened against her legs. Her breasts were magnificent: not just plump but heavy, breasts that would overflow a man's hands.

He glanced over, catching the gleaming eyes of a man ogling Daisy's body. Miles's blood went cold as he drew her close enough that she was obscured from his gaze.

The man stepped sideways. "Good evening, Miss Wharton. I hope to escort you to supper."

"Good evening, Mr. Hemlock," Daisy said. "May I introduce you to Lord Devin?"

"Evening. The answer is no," Miles told the lout. He spun Daisy away from Hemlock, but unfortunately his foot caught the hem of her skirt, and he heard a distinct ripping sound. He looked down Daisy's back and saw, bared to general view, two generous globes, lightly veiled by a translucent chemise. Enough satin panels had separated from her bodice for her entire rear to be exposed.

He turned her around again, so her back was to the wall. Given Daisy's calm expression, she hadn't registered the ripping sound, nor realized that half her gown was missing.

"What on earth are you doing?" she inquired. She came up on her toes and craned her neck to see over his shoulder. "Mr. Hemlock, perhaps we could dance later this evening."

Miles turned his head and gave the man a deadly glare. Not being an entire fool, Hemlock fell back.

"Yes, later," he exclaimed, skittering away.

"Don't ever dance with him," Miles ordered. "I recognize his name. It was in connection with the Earl of Debbleton's charge for...for..." Too late he realized that he could not inform a young lady precisely what the earl had been accused of, as it was one of the unsavory cases he'd been asked to investigate for the House of Lords.

"I read about it," Daisy said coolly. "The earl built a playhouse with a proscenium stage, the better to personally perform with a hired troupe of actresses. I gather the plays they chose to enact were of an unusual type."

Miles blinked down at her. "Does nothing shock you?"

"The murder of Jeremy Tulip shocked me," Daisy said. "In comparison, the Earl of Debbleton's criminality seems not only trivial but downright dull. Why should I care what he does in the privacy of his own estate?"

"His wife cared."

"Likely she had any number of reasons to be offended," Daisy agreed. "But does that mean their marital problems should occupy the gossip columns? What did Mr. Hemlock have to do with it?"

"He was charged with procurement."

Her brows drew together. It seemed that there was *something* this sophisticated young lady didn't know.

"He allegedly supplied the earl with young women from the provinces who came to London seeking their fortunes but were forced to perform on that particular stage."

She winced. "That's revolting."

"Didn't you say it was merely a private matter?"

"I take your point, Lord Devin. Those poor young women. I shouldn't have ventured an opinion when my knowledge was so shallow."

Daisy had shocked him again. Almost no one of his acquaintance would admit to being wrong. Her uncle, for example, had blustered about his innocence whenever their paths crossed during the murder trial. Miles considered his apoplectic fit the result of outrage when no one agreed with him.

Off to one side, a footman picked up the white satin panels torn from Daisy's gown. He draped them over his arm, likely thinking they made up a lady's shawl, and walked away before Miles could catch his eye.

Jolted by the reminder of precisely why they were standing together, Miles said, "Miss Wharton, I didn't keep you here merely because of Mr. Hemlock's association with Debbleton."

Daisy raised an eyebrow. "I was beginning to wonder, since Lady Regina will be waiting to dine with you. I should find my mother."

"You can't move," Miles said.

"Actually, I must move or *you*, Lord Devin, will find yourself embroiled in a scandal. Perhaps you haven't noticed, but a good half of the ballroom is fascinated by the marked attention you have been paying me this evening. Gossipers are not privy to your horror at that idea and may assume that you are courting me."

"I am not horrified," Miles snapped. In fact, he was shockingly close to announcing his intentions, despite all his best instincts.

She looked up at him with a curious expression, somewhere between skepticism and surprise.

Miles cleared his throat. "Be that as it may, you mustn't leave at this moment."

At that, Daisy's brows drew together. "I have the greatest dislike for orders, Lord Devin. Goodbye." She stepped sideways and turned to go.

Instinctively his eyes dropped to her arse. It was—his arms shot out and caught her, pulling her back against the wall.

"Lord Devin!" Her eyes sparked with anger. "Your behavior is quite unacceptable. We both know that you don't wish to have your name linked with mine. Even if you hadn't said so earlier, I could have surmised that from the condescending remarks that you've made to me over the last year or so. I labeled you my suitor out of pure mischief, to see if you would turn white with fear." She paused. "Which you did."

"You misunderstood."

Daisy shrugged. "I found that idea amusing, but I am no longer amused. I do not wish my name to be linked to yours any more than you wish for the reverse."

In one fluid motion she twisted away from him again, exposing her near-naked bottom to the room. Without thinking, Miles stepped forward and pressed his front directly against her back.

And backside.

Episode 95:
The Humiliation of Exposure

Daisy's first thought was that something thick and long was pressed against her rear. The second thought followed almost instantly: she should not have been able to feel anything, given her voluminous skirts—but without her noticing, those skirts had lightened.

In the rear.

Horror scorched through her as she jolted forward. "My gown!" she squeaked, dropping her fan and slapping her right hand over her bottom.

Sure enough, the satin panels at the back of her dress were missing. She curled her fingers, trying to see whether they were hanging by threads, but no. All the panels in the rear had ripped free. She couldn't feel anything other than her chemise, constructed of handkerchief linen and certainly transparent in this light. She looked down in desperation, but no fabric was puddled at her feet.

Surprise morphed into fear. Daisy felt suddenly dizzy, her gasping breath loud and ragged in her ears. The brightly lit ballroom blurred before her eyes.

Lord Devin's right hand gently curled around her waist. "If you'll forgive me, Miss Wharton." He drew her backward toward the pillar.

Two dowagers not far away were watching them with curiosity; Daisy forced a smile and waved at them gaily as she slid sideways to place her back against the marble once again.

"My skirt is missing panels!" she whispered, flattening her bottom against the cool stone. "Where are they?" She glanced around frantically.

"A footman thought a shawl had dropped and picked them up. I couldn't catch his attention without half the room realizing that the length of satin he was carrying matched your gown," Lord Devin said.

Her mother had insisted that the *modiste* add panel after panel of fabric, which had obviously resulted in the stitching giving way. Daisy took a shuddering breath. She was lucky that the whole skirt hadn't ripped away, leaving her half-naked on the dancefloor.

She leaned her head against the pillar and stared up at the ceiling, trying to calm her breathing. How was it that these things always happened to her? Her mother would undoubtedly say it was due to Daisy's lack of refinement. It was just as well that Lady Wharton was nowhere to be seen because Daisy had a feeling that her mother would fall into a fit of palpitations, calling even more attention to her missing skirts.

"The door is all the way across the floor. How can we get there?" Daisy whispered, realizing that her teeth were chattering—not from a chill, but from fear. "How can *I* get there?" she corrected.

She was ruined. Her poor mother *would* be clothed in sackcloth and ashes. No one would ever stop talking about the moment Miss Wharton's fat bottom was revealed to polite society. It would be bad enough if it were Regina's trim rear... but Daisy's?

"I feel sick," she added.

"I'll walk closely behind you, escorting you to the corridor." Lord Devin's eyes caught hers. "Don't panic, Miss Wharton. You bested the guards at the entrance to the Tower of London, very nearly smuggling a file into Beauchamp Tower. You will stroll across the dance floor pretending that your gown is intact. It's all in your expression. Look insouciant."

Daisy felt as if she couldn't get enough air into her lungs. Lady Regina was somewhere close by. If *she* realized what had happened to Daisy's gown, if she saw... Daisy's mind reeled with ugly comments: "fat and unkempt" would be the least of them.

"Where's your fan?" Lord Devin asked.

Daisy nodded to where it lay on the floor. "Can you please retrieve it?" she asked, wishing it was the size of a barn, so she could hide behind it.

Since the orchestra was taking a break before supper, Lord Devin was able to stroll over and scoop up her fan without dodging dancers. Guests were chattering in small groups, which meant that the two of them standing together didn't look as out of place as they might have been.

He bowed and handed her the fan, his face utterly calm, as if nothing was happening. As if...

Her eyes flew to his pantaloons, which did nothing to disguise a broad length skewing left, almost reaching his waistband.

Lord Devin normally looked at her with arrogance and condescension, as if she were a fool who had strayed into his path.

But now his eyes were hooded. He was standing just in front of her, so close that she could feel the warmth of his body and smell fresh linen. Of course, fresh linen. He was the sort of man who bathed every day. Twice a day, she thought wildly.

Behind him, the chamber was emptying as people drifted toward supper.

"Perhaps we could just stay here until the floor is empty," Daisy suggested, her voice wavering.

He shook his head. "That would draw attention to us."

Everyone had already seen them standing together, but she didn't want to remind him since she needed his help. "That's one thing about you, Lord Devin," she said, before thinking.

"What?"

"You always *help*. You helped my uncle, even though you believed he was a traitor, didn't you?"

"Actually, I didn't think Tyron was clever enough for the subterfuge of coded letters," Lord Devin said with brutal casualness.

"I suppose not," Daisy said. Her chemise was little more than gauze; she had never, ever, thought of her bottom as a sensual part of her body, but it was... It definitely was. Pressing it against the wall under the scrutiny of Lord Devin's dark gaze was making heat pour down her legs like scalding honey.

"If you turn slightly to your left, I will move into position behind you," his lordship said, obviously having no idea of her humiliating response to his closeness. "Open your fan."

"To hold it against my rear? People will notice."

"No, to hide your expression," he said, adding more gently, "You look stricken."

Stricken?

At least she didn't look lustful. Thank God for small favors.

Obediently Daisy turned to her left. He stepped forward, bringing his silk pantaloons into contact with the hand that was vainly trying to cover her bottom. She snatched it away with a gasp.

As his large body crowded behind hers, she drew in a sharp breath. That ... *something* pulsed against her nearly bare bottom.

"I apologize," Lord Devin said in a husky voice. "We are both embarrassingly exposed."

A group of ladies was passing before them, so Daisy lowered her fan and smiled casually, as if Lord Devin was merely escorting her out of the ballroom, albeit while standing abnormally close. The dowagers nodded and continued on.

"Don't you think you should address me as Miles, under the circumstances?" His voice was a smoky thread in her ear. "And I shall address you as Daisy, which is how I have thought of you for months."

She cleared her throat. "Good evening, Lady Shelby!"

The lady walked by, the feathers she wore on her head waggling.

"Miles," Daisy breathed. "Are you—" She ran out of words. Honestly, she wasn't even entirely sure what she wanted to say.

"I've never known you to be at a loss for words before ... *Daisy.*" Amusement was threaded through his voice.

They began moving, strolling across the ballroom toward the door. Unless someone happened to glance at them from the side and saw his body pressed against hers, they might not consider their proximity.

But if they did? He was touching her. An important part of him was—

Daisy cleared her throat again, wondering if she was imagining a sensation that was only in her head. Almost certainly it was.

She had always had a naughty imagination. Other young ladies would probably scream and faint if they caught sight of a naked groom. Even at the age of fourteen, Daisy hadn't screamed. Or fainted.

That particular groom had been completely naked, bathing himself in the horse trough. Standing in the sunlight, pouring a pail of water over his head.

Though she *had* felt faint that night in her bed, thinking...

Whatever was touching her rear was thick and hard; what else could it be besides his private part? Yet perhaps this situation had no relation to her bare bottom. Perhaps men walked around all the time like this, and she simply hadn't noticed, never having been in actual contact with a male body.

That was probably it.

They were almost at the door. She could see a few footmen milling about. Once they reached the entry, she would sink onto a bench, request her pelisse, and refuse to move until it was delivered.

"You seem puzzled. Do you have a question I might answer, Daisy?" Miles asked softly, his breath stirring the curls at her ear.

Any proper young lady would ignore his provocation—because that's what it was. Unless he was just trying to take her attention away from the possible disaster of her rear end being exposed to everyone.

They halted again to allow a flushed and lightheaded countess to progress out of the room before them, leaning on her husband's arm.

"Yes, I do," Daisy said. "I have a question. That is, I have several questions but the most pressing—" She broke off, because he started laughing. She looked back and up at him. "I've never heard you laugh."

"I often laugh." He frowned. "Well, I used to laugh. I've become more somber in recent years. At any rate, your *pressing question*? The answer is yes. Thank goodness you are less shockable than other ladies of my acquaintance. If you feel embarrassed, I assure you that I feel equally disconcerted. I haven't experienced such a lack of control since I was a lad."

Daisy rarely blushed, but now she felt her cheeks turning red. Still, she was dying to know more. "Is the phenomenon in question a daily occurrence? Hourly occurrence?"

She twisted about as another crack of laughter erupted from his lips, frowning at him. "Stop bellowing like that!"

One of his large hands landed on her left hip and pulled her back into alignment—which meant close contact with his body. "Don't move. Good evening again, Lady Regina!"

Episode 96:
The Utility of Codpieces

Regina tripped up to them, eyes shining, her lips curved in a cheerful smile. "Good evening!" she cried. "Shall we go into supper now?"

"I have a wretched headache and must return home," Daisy said. "Lord Devin is escorting me to the entry so that I can sit down while waiting for my mother."

"Oh, do you feel faint?" Regina sounded sympathetic, but she looked eager. "Of course, you must leave. It's all those layers of satin." She flipped open her fan and leaned close. "You must be horribly sweaty. If you don't mind my mentioning it, your face is quite red and blotchy."

The hapless countess had chosen to sink into her husband's arms in the doorway, which was vastly irritating. On the other hand, all the guests were focused on her operatic moans and paying no attention to the way Lord Devin—Miles—was plastered to Daisy's back.

"I suppose it's the heat," Regina continued, closing her fan. "Do you see spots before your eyes, Miss Wharton?"

"She is unsteady on her feet," Miles put in. "Perhaps the heat combined with champagne."

"I didn't drink any champagne!" Daisy protested.

Regina beamed up at Miles. "I wondered why you were being so attentive. Of course you are standing ready to catch Miss Wharton, like a knight in shining armor." She began vigorously waving her fan, presumably to cool Daisy's face.

"Lady Regina, I have been invited to dine at the Duke and Duchess of Trent's table," Miles said. "Would you be so kind as to inform them that I shall join you once Miss Wharton is safely in her mother's care?"

Regina's eyes lit up. "Of course! I shall leave through the other entrance, shall I? Since the countess has been so inconsiderate as to faint in that doorway."

Daisy swallowed hard as Regina trotted away. He...It...*moved*.

"I apologize." Miles's voice was gruff, quite unlike the gentlemanly Lord Devin's usual accent. "I cannot control it, Daisy. No gentleman could, not pressed up against you like this. You are so damned delectable."

Daisy was dying to see his expression, but she was afraid of what hers might reveal. She ought to be horrified, and she didn't trust her own acting abilities to convey disgust. In fact, her face might well show humiliating eagerness.

"I was under the impression that such reactions were reserved for the bedchamber," she said, schooling her voice to a ladylike tenor.

"Generally yes. I am glad not to have shocked you to the marrow, but very occasionally a man does lose control. I suspect that is why my ancestors wore codpieces," Miles said thoughtfully.

"Are you making a joke?"

"Of a sort. I do have a sense of humor."

"Not that I've noticed. At any rate, codpieces make sense." She flipped open her fan and hid behind it again. Her knees were trembling, and every instinct told her to snuggle backward against his body—which would be the most scandalous action of her life.

No one had ever called her delectable before. She didn't think anyone had ever *found* her delectable.

"Just to clarify, you rarely find yourself in this state?" she inquired.

In front of her, the countess was in a fit of full-blown hysterics, and behind her, Miles was laughing so hard that he was likely to convulse as well. "Never. Not at my age," he managed.

"I don't see what's so funny," Daisy observed. "How am I to know such things? I wouldn't have imagined men being plagued by this sort of occurrence, but now I think on it, why else would our ancestors have worn codpieces? Those adornments look so silly, strung with ribbons and bows."

"I expect that the stockings they wore would have revealed far more than modern pantaloons." Miles cleared his throat. "Are you deliberately leaning against me?"

"No!" She jerked forward, but his hand held her in place: close, but not too close.

"I'll be damned if I don't feel as out of control as a lad of fifteen," he rumbled.

Daisy felt a wash of pleasurable happiness spiked with mischief. "Missing your ancestral codpiece, are you?" In a fit of madness, she *did* lean back against him, swallowing a gasp as their bodies connected more firmly.

His hand tightened on her hip. "Did you know that I can look directly down your bodice?"

She straightened. "Really? My mother chose this design with fervent attention to disguising the fleshier parts of my body."

"Why are you wrinkling your nose? Do you not like your figure?"

"This is a silly conversation," Daisy said. "As it happens, I do like my figure."

"As do I."

A wave of happiness washed over her. Miles had never given the impression that he considered her fat and unkempt. The evidence was to the contrary, her mind helpfully suggested. Leaning against him had confirmed it.

She turned her head up and smiled a thank you for his compliment. He had never looked at her with an expression like the one on his face now: amused, desirous, intimate—as far from the chilly lord of her experience as possible.

As if they were not only friends, but lovers.

"I used to make jokes," Miles said, out of the blue.

Daisy blinked and tried to focus on that, rather than her shameless instincts. "What muzzled your sense of humor?"

"Managing investigations for the House of Lords. Most of the cases are dark. Depressing, to be frank."

"Such as my uncle's treason case?"

"You and Frederick made that case more pleasurable."

"That's surprising," Daisy observed. "I thought you found me excruciatingly annoying."

"No."

"Are you certain? Because I am fairly certain that most everyone does."

"What?" He sounded startled.

"Find me annoying." The words rushed out of her mouth. "My cousin is the only person who can bear to be around me for long periods of time. My mother finds me irritating, my father told me once that he flees to the country merely to avoid my chatter, and my uncle loathed me."

"Your uncle." His voice was flat. "If I were you, I would not take his disapprobation as an insult."

"He *did* threaten to throw my cousin overboard," Daisy confessed.

"His own daughter?"

Daisy nodded. "He judged my laughter licentious, so I expect I would have had the same fate as poor Jeremy Tulip had I boarded his ship. Which I never would have done, since I abhorred him," she added. "Our dislike was mutual."

"I applaud your judgment. How did we move to such a sour topic?"

"It stemmed naturally from your deficient sense of humor," Daisy said.

"*You* make me laugh," Miles said.

In front of them, the lady's husband caught her under her arms in an ungainly grasp and dragged her into the foyer.

Daisy let out a relieved sigh. "We can walk again."

Miles shook his head. "Not quite yet." He cleared his throat, easing away from her body. "I would prefer not to shock ladies less worldly than you."

"Lord Devin." She frowned up at him. "I trust that you are not drawing invidious conclusions about me based on this unfortunate accident."

"I apologize for that implication." Their eyes met; his were dark with an expression she found very easy to interpret. "You were to call me Miles," he said, his voice dropping to an even lower register.

Daisy bit her lip, suddenly feeling shy. They talked so easily together, but most of the time she hadn't been looking into his eyes, which were seemingly full of bottomless emotion. Now it felt as if the room fell away, along with her fear of scandal and her trepidation about her mother's health. As if the world shrank to just the two of them.

Her breath caught in her throat because his direct look spoke to something deep and frightening within her. She had shrugged off Lord Devin's derisive statements and scalding looks. She had teased him when he appeared horrified at the idea of wooing her.

But when he was Miles rather than Lord Devin? She felt vulnerable.

Surely this simple conversation couldn't have stolen away her bravado and her immunity. Was it due to the fact he had saved her reputation, or the fact that he desired her?

"I should like to be escorted directly to a bench in the entry, and a footman sent to summon my mother," she said, pulling herself together.

He nodded, the teasing light falling from his eyes. "Of course."

A moment later she dropped onto the bench, which led to the odd sensation of buttoned velvet against her bottom. Miles bowed and kissed her hand, his lips lingering for a second longer than prescribed before he bade her good evening and left to find Lady Wharton.

Daisy's mother didn't appear for a good ten minutes, and then she was clucking with annoyance. "Why must we leave?"

"My gown is ripped."

"A maid can repair your hem," her mother said impatiently. "Lady Castlereigh and I are in the midst of a most curative conversation. All is forgiven and forgotten as far as my brother is concerned."

"Mother," Daisy hissed, "the back of my gown is *gone*."

"What do you mean, 'gone'?"

"It fell off on the dancefloor." She plucked up the panel of satin covering her leg, just enough so that her mother could see her chemise.

"As I live and breathe!" Lady Wharton squealed. Her head whipped left and right. The butler was fully occupied helping a lady put on her pelisse. "It could only happen to you. Other women tear a hem, but you tear off your entire gown."

"The *modiste* warned that the fabric was overly heavy for the bodice," Daisy stated, not in the mood to accept her mother's judgment.

"Did anyone see your shame?" she hissed.

"Almost no one. Since sitting on this bench, I have not moved."

The butler approached with their pelisses. As Daisy stood, her mother craned her neck to see her rear and let out a squeak of dismay.

They were in the carriage before Lady Wharton picked up the topic. "You said *almost* no one saw? Please tell me Lady Regina wasn't in your vicinity. I saw her speaking to you and Lord Devin earlier in the evening. She seems to have set her sights on his lordship, since she was hanging on his arm at the supper table."

Daisy's mouth tightened, but Miles was not hers, no matter how intense the feelings that sprang up between them this evening. "Regina did not see my mishap."

"Who did?"

"Actually, it was Lord Devin. He kindly walked behind me so that no one could see my rear."

"The best possible outcome," her mother declared, somewhat surprisingly. "That man will never tell tales. From what I understand, he knows all the most disreputable secrets of the peerage, but he never gossips. I shall discreetly thank him tomorrow."

Daisy raised an eyebrow. "Tomorrow?"

"Lady Castlereigh has invited us to join her at a dinner in honor of her nephew's betrothal to Lord Devin's sister Clementine," her mother said proudly. "Lord Devin will be in attendance, of course."

Daisy dropped her gaze just in time to conceal the blaze of joy that went through her.

"I suspect that Lord Devin feels partially responsible for your uncle's absence in your life," Lady Wharton mused. "After all, his apoplexy was the direct result of the investigation he led."

Daisy believed her uncle's death was ultimately caused by his sheer outrage, stemming from the fear that he—a member of the peerage—might actually be convicted.

"This evening Lady Castlereigh made such a wise observation," her mother continued. "In the Bible, God asks Cain where Abel is, and he says, 'Am I my brother's keeper?' The answer is no, of course he is not."

Daisy frowned. "I think the import of that verse is the opposite. Cain was supposed to care about Abel's whereabouts."

"Nonsense! I trust you are not setting yourself up to disagree with the biblical interpretations of a *peer of the realm*! It took you forever merely to learn to read. Why, you must have been five years old by the time you mastered your ABCs."

She leaned over and patted Daisy's knee. "Not that I blame you for that sluggishness. You learned how to read in the end, and that's all that matters. Lady Castlereigh says..."

Daisy stopped listening. Miles had instructed her to call him by his first name—did that mean they were courting? Perhaps he would pay her a call tomorrow morning or ask her to go for a drive in Hyde Park.

He didn't find her fat and unkempt. He said she was sophisticated. He thought she was funny.

More importantly, he wanted her. The more Daisy thought about it, the more certain she was that he would pay a call tomorrow morning.

She went to sleep with a smile on her lips.

Episode 97:
A Decent Proposal

Miles rose the next morning with a sense of inevitability. He was a gentleman who came from a long line of honorable men. Having seen Miss Wharton's unclothed rear, he was obligated to propose marriage. Caught in the parson's mousetrap.

Daisy would soon become Lady Devin.

His future wife was flighty, impulsive, silly...

And intelligent, witty, and self-possessed. She hadn't panicked in a situation when many young women would have collapsed in a faint—or pretended to do so.

Not that it mattered.

More crucially, she was *his*. The moment she leaned teasingly back against him, and then giggled... Or perhaps it was the moment when her eyes grew larger as her bottom pressed against the ballroom wall.

She was his.

Staring unthinkingly at the mirror, he twisted his cravat in the complicated folds of formal dress. Lady Wharton would expect him to be dressed as one would be for the queen's drawing room.

Maybe Daisy had been his from the moment he strode across Lord Rothingale's ballroom and saw hair spilling like moonlight from beneath a masquerade hat.

"Congratulate me, Stubbins," he said to his valet. "I'm planning to ask for a young lady's hand in marriage."

"She's a lucky woman," Stubbins said cheerfully. His valet had been his father's manservant and had known Miles since he was a lad.

"I hope she agrees with you."

Daisy had looked at him with desire. She had trembled against him, and not just because of shock. She had *nestled* against him.

He was hers.

An hour later, he was disabused of that notion.

"Absolutely not," Lady Wharton said. She held up her hand, palm toward him. "And do not imagine that an appeal to my husband will make any difference, Lord Devin. I hold the purse strings, and Lord Wharton gave up responsibility for our daughter long ago."

Miles felt a violent wish to disobey the lady's command. If need be, he could elope with Daisy, though the resulting scandal would be irritating.

"You don't think that your daughter should be consulted as regards her marriage?" he inquired, keeping his tone mild.

She snorted. "My daughter is far too young and innocent to be able to understand what it means to marry a man of your reputation."

"My reputation?" His voice chilled.

"All those women," she said grimly. "Don't try to tell me you're not a rakehell, because I've heard stories from numerous sources."

"I have done nothing that other men of my rank have not," he said, startled into defending himself. "I don't even have a mistress."

"But you have had," she snapped. "Aye, and you've frequented the opera enough. I've heard all about your *penchant* for Russian opera dancers and their ilk. You have extremely low standards."

"Do you mean to be so insulting?" Miles asked. If she were a man, he'd challenge her. But she wasn't. She was an enraged mother lion, determined to protect her cub.

"You continue to be friends with Rothingale!" Lady Wharton screeched. "The rogue very nearly eloped with your own sister, Clementine. 'Tis a miracle that she's now betrothed." Her lip curled. "If men of Clementine's own family are not interested in defending her virtue, the least they could do would be to give the reprobate the cut direct. But you? You continue to *consort* with him!"

She wasn't saying anything that Miles hadn't considered. "What if I mend my reputation? I take your point about Rothingale."

"Don't do it for Daisy's sake," she said acidly. "I will *never* marry my daughter to a man as old as you are."

That was a facer. "I'm not yet thirty, and my understanding is that Daisy is in her twenties as well."

"Daisy will marry a man who's not yet twenty-five." The lady's cheeks were marked with red slashes. "Regardless, you should feel an *avuncular* sentiment for her, if anything! After all, you are partially responsible for the lack of an uncle in her life."

Fury was creeping up Miles's spine. He was *not* old. Neither was he dissolute.

"Don't you *dare* think of trying to elope with Daisy, the way that wastrel tried to do with your sister," Lady Wharton shrilled, getting to her feet. "Disgusting old men who seduce young ladies will never be sanctioned by me!"

Miles rose to his feet. He had never met Lady Wharton's husband, but he understood the gentleman to be some twenty years older than his wife. He was beginning to think that their marriage began with a rash elopement.

"I'll have your vow on that front!" she demanded.

Right.

Well, he hadn't been entirely convinced that he wished to marry Daisy anyway.

"I will not elope with your daughter," he stated. "If you'll excuse me, Lady Wharton, I'll be on my way."

"You're taking this suspiciously well," she spat.

"I witnessed the catastrophe of Miss Wharton's gown. In the process of saving her reputation, I glimpsed her in a state of dishabille. My honor and hers demanded that I offer my hand."

Lady Wharton's countenance cleared. "You must forgive me, Lord Devin."

He blinked at her toothy smile. "Pardon me?"

"My vehement rejection of your proposal was inappropriate. I've noticed that men do have a tendency to fall in love with Daisy, due to her vivacious mannerisms—I am determined to guide her into more subdued behavior this Season, mind you—but now I understand that is not the case here."

Miles hated the idea of a "subdued" Daisy as much as he hated that blasted dress that looked like a pillar of salt, but it was not his business.

Lady Wharton came closer and patted his arm. "Your reputation may be less than sterling, but you *are* a gentleman, so of course you were compelled to propose after that unfortunate mishap. I expect you are deeply relieved to receive my response. I imagine that you feel my daughter is far too impulsive and silly for you. I would have said as much myself."

He cleared his throat. "I consider Miss Wharton entirely suitable." He stepped back and bowed. "I do thank you for reminding me that boyhood friendship is no reason to acknowledge Lord Rothingale. I shall eschew his company from now on."

"Excellent!" her ladyship said, starting toward the drawing room door in her hurry to see the back of him.

"Good day," Miles said at the door.

"What a shock that was," Lady Wharton chattered. "I believe I must lie down. We shall see you tonight at dinner—" she narrowed her eyes "—where you will make it quite clear to Daisy that you have no interest in her beyond friendly concern stemming from her disturbing experience."

Miles was beginning to feel like a marionette, but he bowed yet again. "As you wish."

That evening Daisy maddened her mother by refusing to wear one of her new gowns, the ones that swathed her in fabric.

Instead she chose a slightly-out-of-date dress made of amber-colored silk with turquoise spangled trim. The fabric floated around her hips and flirted with her ankles. Her curves were enhanced by short stays, but not compressed by them, and the trimming turned her eyes cornflower blue.

"I suppose it's acceptable for dinner," Lady Wharton finally said, giving up. "I doubt that any marriageable young men are invited."

"Lord Devin will be there," Daisy said, turning around before the mirror and tugging on the back of her gown, just in case. It was firmly sewn in place.

Did she look delectable? Hopefully. Her hair was caught up with amber silk ribbons, with one thick coil placed just so over her shoulder.

"Lord Devin is too old for you," Lady Wharton stated. "Your father's age has always been a barrier between us."

"Yes, but Father is twenty years older than you are," Daisy observed.

"You may marry a man three years older than you *at the most.*"

Daisy kept her mouth shut; her mother would surely change her mind if Lord Devin—one of the richest and most eligible bachelors in London—began paying marked attention to her daughter.

Every time she thought about Miles's eyes, dazzling possibilities sprang alive in her mind. Ones where she married the man who had told her not to move lest he'd shock polite society, and who had sucked in a desperate breath when she disobeyed and leaned back against him.

Except...

As it turned out, Miles didn't even look at her.

He paid her no attention at all.

When she and her mother walked into the drawing room, Daisy's eyes went directly to where he was standing with his sister Clementine.

Their hostess, Lady Castlereigh, hurried toward the door, hands outstretched in greeting, but Miles didn't stir. His eyes cut in their direction, and then he turned directly back to his conversation. In the candlelight, his face was chiseled as if shaped from stone, except no marble angel had a brow so disdainful.

Daisy swallowed hard. He was wearing an exquisite coat of dove-gray silk adorned with black embroidery at the hem and cuffs. He looked far too elegant for someone like her, whose hair already felt as if it might topple to one side.

Perhaps Miles didn't want to make a show of his attention? After all, gossips had seen them together at the ball, even if no one had glimpsed her ripped garment.

But a leaden feeling in her stomach suggested that he didn't wish to pay her attention at all. He'd rethought the prospect of marrying her—if he'd even considered it. He was tall and dignified; she was short and plump, with fly-away hair and a snub nose. Her own mother thought she was a giddy fool.

When Daisy arrived at that end of the room, her heart beating in her ears, Miles bowed with punctilious briskness. "Lady Wharton, it is a pleasure to see you again so soon. And your daughter, of course."

Her mother surged forward and patted him on the arm. "You were quite the gentleman last evening, Lord Devin. Thank you for rescuing Daisy from an embarrassing situation."

"Oh dear," Clementine said, grimacing. "What happened?"

"My gown ripped," Daisy said.

"My brother is quite experienced with such rescues," Clementine said sympathetically. "My family still tells tales of my older sister's debut ball, when the Prince Regent trod on her hem and tore the ruffle clean off! Miles saved the day by sweeping her away before anyone noticed."

"Precisely as he did for Daisy!" Lady Wharton cried. "How I wish that my daughter had an older brother like him. Thankfully, Lord Devin fulfilled the role last night. I expect it comes naturally to him."

Older brother?

"I am partially responsible for the lack of an uncle in Miss Wharton's life," Miles said with sardonic emphasis. "I assure you, Lady Wharton, that I feel avuncular concern for your daughter."

Daisy's heart plummeted to her toes.

"Avuncular!" Clementine tapped Miles on the shoulder with her fan. "You *are* becoming more like a stuffy uncle every day." She turned to Daisy and Lady Wharton. "My brother has changed so much since he took on that awful position in the House of Lords. I promise that he used to be cheerful."

Avuncular.

The word went around in Daisy's head without making much sense, but then she was never very good at vocabulary questions.

He hadn't felt avuncular yesterday, when his cock was throbbing against her bottom.

Miles bowed. "Please excuse me. Lady Regina has arrived, and I should greet her."

The moment he walked away, Clementine said, "If my brother marries Regina, I shall be *so* disappointed."

"It would be an appropriate match," Lady Wharton said. "She must be nearing twenty-five."

"Age is not everything," Daisy said.

If Miles had wanted her, he'd obviously changed his mind. Perhaps he found her too annoying. A feeling of dread sank in as she remembered babbling about that possibility.

He hadn't denied it.

"I hoped to see your younger sisters," Daisy's mother said to Clementine. "While they are not formally out, I thought they might attend a family gathering of this nature."

"It's the most unfortunate thing! Augusta came down with an influenza. She's been frightfully ill for weeks. My brother sent them to live in Bath with an elderly aunt for a few months, until Augusta regains her health."

"Will Catrina and Augusta debut together next year?" Lady Wharton asked.

"I expect so." Clementine brightened. "If you'll excuse me, I would like to introduce Daisy to my fiancé's cousin." She waved toward a lean, bespectacled fellow. "He's a professor at Oxford and very intelligent!"

"Excellent," Lady Wharton said. "Fancy that. A professor, at such a young age!"

Episode 98:
A Bolt from the Blue

A month later, Daisy found herself gripped by two equally embarrassing emotions.

The first was a wild curiosity about the metamorphosis of gentlemen's private parts. She almost wrote her cousin a letter about it but concluded that Livie would probably not care to comment on her husband's "tool," as *City of Eros* called it.

Thanks to the current fashion's requirement for skintight silk pantaloons, Daisy had confirmed that gentlemen found her curves enticing. When allowed to stand close to her, the younger ones in particular seemed to respond. For the sake of experimentation, she allowed one of her more assiduous suitors several kisses and a passionate embrace; a glance from behind her fan afterward had revealed no change in his silhouette, suggesting that Lord Cropley desired her dowry, not her person.

With her wretched luck, Miles had walked by just as she'd emerged from an alcove with Cropley in tow. His eyes went from her reddened lips to her hair, which was falling from her topknot. His demeanor was so chilly that humiliation zinged to Daisy's toes.

Perhaps he couldn't imagine marrying someone as disorderly as she. Or maybe he thought she was dissolute? The self-hating possibilities were dizzying, even though she fiercely reminded herself that Miles had sauntered into Rothingale's masquerade looking for a woman. By rights, she should shudder and turn away every time he entered her view.

That fact together with his disdain made her second obsession even more embarrassing.

She couldn't stop looking for Miles, no matter how much she scolded herself in private. Thrilled by society's open-hearted embrace, Lady Wharton insisted on going out every single night of the week. Sometimes her zeal led to a full day's socializing: a morning champagne breakfast, followed by a matinee at the theater, followed by an evening ball.

Wherever they went, Daisy looked for a tall man with indifferent eyes. They often encountered each other since he was the *crème de la crème* of bachelors and she was one of the most courted women of the Season.

No sooner did he stroll into a ballroom than her heart would thump and her cheeks turn pink, whether or not they exchanged a word. If they happened to be in proximity, he would greet her, but with patent disinterest.

She invariably tried to force him to laugh, and every time she achieved so much as a quirk of his lips, she felt a bolt of pure happiness.

Yet she couldn't fool herself into thinking that he showed any interest. He would dance with her once or twice, but he never leaned against the wall and stared at her broodingly. In fact, he didn't look at her at all unless they were face to face.

The opposite was more true: *she* had to stop herself from staring across the ballroom at *him*. It was mortifying to be in the throes of such a ferocious infatuation.

Her obsession made her indifferent to her suitors—which had the effect of making her all the more attractive to them. She quickly gathered a large circle of admirers, and to her mother's delight, it became clear that Daisy would have her pick of London's bachelors alongside the yet-unattached Lady Regina.

"Rather odd," Regina confided, her eyes wide and innocent, "given that we have such different figures."

"We both have sizable dowries," Daisy pointed out.

Because Regina had all the sensitivity of a cow, she made a jest about the daughter of the Mayor of London, whose dowry was twice the size of theirs. And yet Daisy found herself pitying Regina: her biting comments frightened off as many men as her wealth and status as a duke's daughter attracted.

Why couldn't Daisy have fallen in love with one of the extremely nice gentlemen who genuinely liked her? But her heart was stubbornly stuck on a man who showed no sign of courtship.

One morning as Daisy was making her way to the breakfast room, determined that today she would ignore Miles altogether, the knocker thumped. Since their butler, Mr. Tangle, was nowhere to be seen, she opened the front door expecting to see a liveried groom holding a posy or an invitation—but no one was to be seen. She gazed out at the street for a moment before she glanced down and let out an audible yelp.

A baby.

Right there, on the top step, was a baby girl in a basket, perhaps a few months old. The child was fast asleep, nestled in a satin-trimmed blanket. Her head was ringed in white-blonde curls, and she had a snub nose.

Daisy looked around again before she bent down. "What on earth are you doing here?"

The sound of her own voice brought her back to her senses with a crash. The more relevant question was: *who are you?*

Given that Daisy might have been looking at a breathing portrait of herself as a babe, the answer was not going to be welcome.

"Bloody hell!" she whispered hoarsely, looking yet again at the empty street before she snatched the basket and backed into the entry.

When she pushed the front door closed, the child startled awake. Daisy placed the basket on the floor and crouched beside it.

She had blue eyes. *Daisy* had blue eyes.

Since Daisy definitely hadn't given birth in the last few months, this child...

Her heart sank.

The baby smiled, wide and guileless, her eyes shining. She had one darling tooth in the front of her mouth. "Moo, moo!" A small hand waved in the air before wrapping around one of Daisy's fingers.

"Moo to you too," Daisy crooned. "You are a sweetheart, aren't you? I wonder what your name is?" She didn't see a letter, but surely no mother would desert her child without some sort of message.

"What on earth are you doing?"

Daisy whipped her head about. Her mother was poised at the top of the stairs, looking down with an expression of pure horror. Daisy sprang to her feet. "Mother, perhaps you should sit down. Or rather, come downstairs and then sit down."

"Is that a basket of fruit or a child?" Lady Wharton's tones were frigid. She showed no signs of imminent hysterics, but of course, she hadn't seen the baby. She didn't realize that it was almost certainly a member of the family.

So to speak.

Picking up the basket, Daisy walked into the drawing room and sat down, placing the child at her feet. Her mother deserved privacy during this painful realization, and Tangle might emerge from the breakfast room at any second.

The child was kicking her blanket, trying to free herself. "Moo, moo, moo!" she crowed.

Lady Wharton closed the drawing room door and leaned back against it as if a horde of soldiers were threatening to break in. She cleared her throat. "Where did that come from?" Her words emerged staccato, like the raps of drumsticks.

"She is a baby girl, some months old, and she was on the doorstep."

"It does not belong here." Her voice was uncompromising.

"Someone left her for us to find," Daisy said, trying to find the right words. "Mother, won't you please come look at her?"

"No. I prefer to summon Tangle to remove it."

Daisy frowned. "Surely you agree that we must discover the child's mother." She began feeling around the basket, trying to find a letter.

The child caught hold of her sleeve and babbled some more. She was plump and happy, presumably loved and well cared for.

"Darling girl," Daisy whispered, "something must tell us who you are." She picked up the baby and popped her into the crook of her arm, the better to look under the blanket.

"Moo!"

"I would have protected you from this knowledge," her mother said heavily, walking toward them. "She's one of my husband's by-blows. There's no doubt about it."

Daisy had already reached that conclusion. She cleared her throat. "In that case, my father might..."

"Lord Wharton will either have no idea of the mother's name or dishonestly claim as much," her mother said, folding her arms and staring down at the child.

"This is not the first baby to land on our doorstep, Daisy."

Episode 99:
A Reputation like a Cesspit

*D*aisy could scarcely believe that her elderly father engaged in activities that would lead to a child, let alone a child born to a woman other than her mother. "Excuse me?"

"The first such child arrived within a month of your birth. Did you never wonder why you had no siblings? Why your father had no heir? Why he resides with us only rarely?"

Frankly, Daisy had been under the impression that her parents heartily disliked each other, which would naturally curtail the arrival of more children.

"Suppressing my maternal instincts, I never allowed the man into my bed again." Her mother raised her chin, looking like the marble statue of Queen Britannia in front of St. Paul's Cathedral, ready to martyr herself for her nation. "I sacrificed the siblings you might have had in order to protect both of us from the ignominy of your father's character."

"My goodness." The baby was tugging at her hair, so Daisy began disentangling her fingers. "I never longed for siblings, given that Livie grew up with me in the nursery."

"Livie's mother, my sister-in-law, is a version of my husband. No one knows who Livie's father is, but it was certainly not Sir Tyron."

Daisy gasped. "But you told Livie—"

"I lied to Livie," her mother snapped. "Your cousin would likely have turned down a perfectly good proposal on the grounds of her illegitimacy. I am surrounded by degenerates. My detestable brother married one, and I married another." She sat down in an armchair with a thump, as if her knees suddenly gave way.

"I'm so sorry." Daisy hesitated. "I gather that I have sisters or brothers, other than this one?"

"They are *not* your sisters or brothers," her mother said, her voice grating. "They are by-blows of your father's. Like everything unpleasant in his life, they are left for me to get rid of." She raised a hand. "Don't look at me like that, Daisy!"

"I am not looking at you in any particular fashion," Daisy said, nestling the baby more snugly into the crook of her arm. "It's just hard to understand."

"I do not hold with blaming the child, but neither will I raise my husband's bastards under my roof." Lady Wharton's shoulders slumped. "That's why I took in Livie. I could save one such child. I raised her far from her dissolute mother, and Livie's sweet nature and excellent marriage have rewarded all my efforts."

Daisy's hands trembled as she wrapped the blanket closer around her sister's legs—because the little girl *was* her sister. A sudden memory came back to her: a childhood blanket, soft pale pink wool with a silk border. "I had a blanket like this, didn't I?"

"I expect," her mother said dismissively. "I hope you're not making the mistake of thinking that the child's mother is indigent, Daisy. I'm certain that she profited from your father's attention."

"What happened to the other children?" Daisy was barely able to choke out the question, but she had to know.

"I sent them to the Chelsea Orphanage, accompanied by fifty pounds each for maintenance, and I will do the same with this one," her mother said heavily. "If the child is not adopted by the age of seven, I shall pay another fifty pounds to the Asylum for Female Orphans established by Sir John Fielding, where she will be taught a decent trade."

At seven?

Daisy pulled the child closer, cuddling her protectively. Her mind was reeling. "The baby's mother will miss her dreadfully. Wouldn't it be better to give her money so she might raise her daughter herself?"

"The child is old enough to be weaned, so her mother brought it here, knowing that we would ensure her daughter had a better life than her own—just as I removed Livie from her home, and for the same reason," Lady Wharton added, more gently.

Daisy swallowed hard. She and her cousin had always been told that Livie's mother was too ill to raise her daughter.

"That child's mother is likely a resident of one of the better sort of brothels. To the best of my knowledge, your father does not parley with nightwalkers."

"Nightwalkers?"

"Women who walk the streets of London at night. You seem to know the definition of a brothel, Daisy, which affirms my belief that—"

"But Father lives in the country!" Daisy interrupted.

"Lord Wharton also has a London residence," her mother stated, her expression suggesting that she had caught the whiff of a sewer. "He maintains a bachelor apartment in the Albany. I pay him to live apart from us, and I gather he finds the company of similarly debauched men to be congenial."

Daisy felt this revelation like a physical blow. "How can that be?" she breathed. "Father has an apartment in town? We see him so rarely."

"He dislikes society, and society dislikes him. I dislike him. He, on the other hand, never met a courtesan whom he didn't like, which has led to at least three or four children born out of wedlock."

The baby caught Daisy's hair again, so she used that as an excuse not to look up. She couldn't be surprised by the fact that her father's aversion to polite society extended to his only legitimate daughter. She saw him rarely even when they visited the country, and he'd never hidden how irritating he found her chatter.

"Your father's reluctance to accept his responsibilities has nothing to do with you, Daisy," her mother said. "He loves you as much as he is capable, but he has never grown up. Think of him as perpetually young, convinced that the world will take care of any problems that come his way."

Obviously, "the world" was Lady Wharton. No wonder her mother was so embittered.

"That child's name, by the way, is likely Belle, as I see it embroidered onto her blanket. I suppose her mother is one of the Frenchwomen who escaped the war in Paris. I understand that the better brothels employ hussies from that country."

The words filtered into Daisy's head and then came into focus like a slap of cold water to the face. Her mother's disdain for women fleeing a war-torn country set her teeth on edge, but she put that aside for the moment.

"Do you think more children have been born who were not brought to this doorstep?"

"Almost certainly. I consider it a great misfortune that Lord Wharton's hair color breeds so true. Anyone who saw that child in proximity to you would recognize your common features."

Belle squealed, catching another lock of Daisy's white-blonde hair and chortling as strands ran through her chubby fingers.

"You needn't look so woebegone," her mother observed. "Why do you think I don't allow dissolute old men to propose to you? As a girl, I was fooled by Lord Wharton, but I quickly learned that he had married me only to repair his estate, a fact that did not translate to loyalty on his part. Younger men are more malleable. You may not be able to command fidelity, but the fact that I will leave you my estate should ensure reasonable civility."

"I see."

"I am always looking out for your best interests. The last thing I want is for you to end up in a situation like mine." Lady Wharton's voice rasped. "I have rejected *all* men who resemble your father, such as Lord Devin."

Daisy's head swung up. "What about Lord Devin?"

"Older than you and a reputation like a cesspit," her mother said promptly. "Thoroughly debauched. He regularly frequents places of ill repute."

"Truly?" Daisy asked weakly, though she already knew that to be true. Miles hadn't been wearing a mask at the Rothingale masquerade. He had been prowling around the ballroom, boldly looking for a night's entertainment.

"*I* had to tell him to cut his friendship with Lord Rothingale, a lecherous miscreant who attempted to elope with the man's own sister! It shows Lord Devin's disdain for civilized behavior, given that a woman who is not even a relative had to point out such a salient fact."

"Wait," Daisy said, the context suddenly dawning on her. "Are you saying that Lord Devin offered to marry me?"

"Only because he witnessed your ripped gown. I'll give him that—he responded as a gentleman and showed up the following morning with a lackluster proposal. I turned him down, of course. I will *never* countenance you ending up in a marriage like mine. If only my mother had cared for me as I care for you!"

"You shouldn't have refused him," Daisy blurted out. "At the very least, you should have let me know that he had proposed."

Her mother's lip curled. "What if you had been seduced by his rakish ways? Do you want your marriage to include the odd baby dropped on your doorstep?"

"I should have liked to make the choice."

"Once upon a time, I made a choice between an urbane, sophisticated older man and a fresh-faced puppy ... "

Her mother went on, but Daisy stopped listening. Miles had proposed to her. She felt again the heat of his body behind her, the desire in his eyes, the temptation in his deep voice.

A sharp contrast to the indifferent, sardonic glances she had received from him in the last weeks.

Happiness welled up in her—and dissipated just as quickly. She truly didn't want to marry a man whose children were sprinkled around the country like unwanted kittens. With a shiver, she realized that Belle's existence implied that discarded children could be found everywhere, one of the many secrets kept from young ladies.

Looking down at her sister, she decided that her infatuation with Lord Devin was over. As dead as her innocence.

"Therefore, I refused his request for your hand," Lady Wharton concluded.

"Mother, I cannot relinquish Belle to an orphanage. She is my sister." Daisy leaned down to kiss the baby's forehead. The baby had stuck her thumb in her mouth, but she took it out and gave Daisy a sunny smile.

"Nonsense," her mother snapped. "Use your head, Daisy! I know you're impulsive but try not to be so foolish. That child looks just like you. Your suitors will dissolve into air like cloud castles if gossip spreads about her parentage. Since we were excluded from society last year, we can't point to your ongoing presence at social events to protect your reputation."

"We could tell the truth," Daisy suggested.

"Tell the truth?" Her mother's voice rose. "That my innocent daughter is sheltering a doxy's offspring?" She let out a fierce bark of laughter. "At least now people assume that your father and I are merely ill-disposed to live together, not that he blatantly betrays his marriage vows on a weekly basis."

"We could hide Belle on the third floor, in the nursery," Daisy said. "We could dye her hair with walnut juice."

Her mother snorted. "Absolutely not."

Daisy's mind spun helplessly. "We could send her to the country estate, to the care of a good woman."

"Gossip would spread like wildfire, and believe me, everyone would suspect that the child was yours. It's your future or hers, and she is *not my daughter.*"

"I understand, but—"

Lady Wharton surged to her feet again. "Do you have any idea how mortifying this is for me? You dare ask me to nurture evidence of my husband's betrayal?"

Daisy held her mother's gaze; not for nothing had she grown up in the shadow of a woman strong enough to exile her own spouse. "I can only imagine, and I'm so sorry. However, that doesn't change my opinion regarding Belle."

"This is not merely a matter of your reputation, but *my* well-being. I have had enough affronts for one lifetime. Do you dare to think that I should have raised my husband's bastards? Lived with daily evidence of his infidelity, his lack of respect for me, his poor moral fiber?"

Daisy rocked Belle back and forth, watching her eyelashes flutter. "I'm so sorry that Father neglects his responsibilities."

"I have been sorry for years," her mother said, falling back into her chair. "My regrets don't change reality."

"Moo," the baby said sleepily. Her eyelashes lay on her cheeks like tiny fans.

"I cannot give her away," Daisy said desperately. "I cannot."

"You must. Thankfully, Tangle is both experienced and discreet. He will deliver her himself, rather than trust a groom. He will make certain that the Chelsea Orphanage understands that she is to be well cared for."

"Children are often hungry and cold, even in the best orphanages," Daisy insisted. "No one plays with them or even speaks to them. They are left in cribs for the whole day. When they are older, they are put to work for hours, sometimes in the sleet and snow."

"Not in the Chelsea Orphanage. She will grow up surrounded by children who also have noble blood, albeit diluted. It is the best such establishment in the city, one where young ladies of quality volunteer, obviously without having any idea that they might be related to one of the orphans."

"But you never allowed me—" Daisy broke off.

Her mother nodded. "How could I allow you to volunteer with other girls, given that your father's bastards resemble you so closely? I made up a story about Livie's mother not approving of the activity, as if that woman cared a fig for what her daughter did from day to day!"

Daisy felt dangerously close to tears. "I see."

"Your hair is so unusual, as is that child's," Lady Wharton said. "If you want to blame someone, blame your father."

"But—"

"I don't mean to be unkind, but it is time to *grow up*," she interrupted, hoisting herself out of the chair as if she were an arthritic old woman. "Your girlhood is over."

"I—" Daisy began, but her mother cut her off again.

"Your father has never accepted the fact that what people think matters." Her lips twisted. "He goes his sweet way, regardless of the consequences for others. I refuse to allow you to resemble him in that. I have built a life, a life that matters, by respecting the consequences of my actions. Do you understand?"

Daisy couldn't stop looking at Belle's face. Given the delicacy of her bone structure, her mother must be incredibly beautiful.

"I had to talk Lady Castlereigh around to forgiving me for my brother's criminality. Without her approval, you would have no suitors at all. None. My position in society was rocked by Sir Tyron's criminal actions, but not destroyed. But *you*? My own daughter? If you are suspected of behaving like a hussy, I will have no further place in society."

Daisy's heart sank like a stone.

"You have been testing me since you turned thirteen years of age," her mother said flatly. "You made your disrespect obvious every time you stole out of this house unaccompanied by a maid."

A sharp pain twisted in Daisy's chest. "I didn't mean to be disrespectful."

"Do you think that I was unaware that you and your cousin were galloping in Hyde Park last year? That *somehow* she met Major FitzRoy, though they were never introduced in my presence?" She snorted. "You have a mutinous strain, likely inherited from your wretched father. I am willing to accept that you can't help yourself, but you cannot ruin my life!"

Daisy swallowed hard and whispered, "I can't send Belle to that place." A sob struggled up her throat.

Lady Wharton's frown deepened. "Do you think I allowed myself to cry when I discovered that baby on my doorstep when you were first born? Or when my brother's wife birthed a child in his absence?"

"No?"

"Grow up, Daisy!" she repeated. "No whining. No malingering. I rescued Livie. I paid for the other children, and I continue to pay for them. We do *what we can*."

"I understand."

That didn't mean that she agreed.

"I have a terrible headache, so I shall retire to my room," her mother declared. "Tangle will take the child, and I trust you will not make a fuss about it."

Daisy drew in a shuddering breath.

"She cannot be seen by anyone, from a groom to a maid," Lady Wharton continued, heading toward the door. "I shall tell him to retrieve her immediately." The door closed behind her.

Grow up?

As Daisy understood it, maturity involved making ethical decisions rather than allowing others to dictate one's choices. She may have spent her life irritating her mother, but she rarely directly contradicted her.

Now? That mutinous inheritance from her father was in full swing.

Sending a relative to an orphanage due to shame or rage—both emotions she completely understood and sympathized with—was not right.

Belle wasn't her mother's blood relation, though.

She was Daisy's.

In all senses of the word but one, this child was Daisy's.

Episode 100:
Of Lechers and Bastards

Belle made an anxious sound and pulled at Daisy's hair again. "Moo?" Daisy pulled out a handkerchief and dried her eyes. "Moo," she agreed, her voice cracking. Then she placed the baby back into the basket, tucking the blanket around her. Belle immediately began sucking her thumb.

"We can't stay here," she said aloud, her mind scrambling as she tried to think of solutions. If she had garnered one thing from the painful conversation with her mother, it was that Lady Wharton was desperate to keep her place in society. If Daisy raised Belle, her mother would be summarily abandoned by her friends.

So Belle had to be raised elsewhere. Her father didn't care about his illegitimate offspring, so trying to find him would do no good.

Two people came to mind: Frederick and Miles.

She was enormously fond of Frederick, but he wasn't a hedonist, the way Miles was. Daisy doubted very much that Frederick had ever been in a house of ill-repute—if only because he was infamous for bedding married women. She had a shrewd feeling that he had no lover at the moment. He was technically courting her, after all, albeit in an inebriated and lackadaisical fashion.

Thus Frederick likely hadn't fathered a bastard child.

But Miles? She could readily imagine him strolling through a brothel on the arm of an elegant Frenchwoman. The memory of him smiling down at her at the Rothingale masquerade when he believed she was a courtesan gave her a burning sensation in the back of her throat.

She didn't want *that* in a husband. She didn't want *him*.

She owed her mother an apology. Lady Wharton was right. Better to marry a greenhorn, one of the young boys who clustered about her at dances, than a man whose taste for depravity was bred in the bone.

In fact, she'd prefer to marry Frederick—better a drunk rather than a lecher. A grim choice, but salutary. "Growing up" involved hard choices.

Yet if Miles and her father were both lechers, they were cut from different cloth. She refused to believe that Miles would dispatch his illegitimate offspring to an orphanage, even the best such establishment in London.

Rakehell he may be, but he was a decent man. His by-blows were surely housed somewhere in the country where they were loved and cared for, perhaps on his own estate. She straightened, thinking hard. If Belle joined Miles's offspring, no one would ever make a connection between Daisy and the child.

Miles was *kind*. He was a problem-solver. He would understand that Belle had to be kept safe from society's reproach. What's more, if Miles took her in, Daisy could see occasionally see her sister. Somehow.

Tangle would appear at any moment, a thought that propelled Daisy to her feet. She pulled her fichu from the neckline of her gown and draped it over Belle's basket, arranging it so lace hung over the sides as if she were carrying a gift of fruit from the country. Then she walked straight out the door.

At the end of the block, she peeked under the fichu and discovered Belle was still sucking her thumb, albeit with her eyes closed. The baby would probably need to be fed fairly soon; Daisy had the vague understanding that babies had to be fed numerous times a day.

Suddenly she remembered that Miles's sister Clementine was a terrible gossip. Perhaps she should announce herself under a false name to ensure that Clementine never learned of her visit. That seemed like an excellent precaution.

She had resolved to introduce herself as one of her favorite theatrical characters and was walking quickly toward Miles's house when she ran into Lady Regina.

"Good morning, Miss Wharton!"

"Lady Regina!" Daisy caught herself. "I mean, good morning, Lady Regina."

"What on earth are you doing at my end of the street? For my part, I am taking an early constitutional. I find that taking three or four walks a day is critical for maintaining my figure." Regina waved dismissively at her maid, who dropped back to stand out of earshot. "Where on earth is your maid? I might have assumed you were a servant delivering fresh bread if I hadn't recognized your gown. I *do* like that fringe. It's from Quimby's Emporium, is it not?"

"Yes, it is," Daisy replied. "If you'll forgive me, Lady Regina, I must drop this basket off and dash home. My mother would be most displeased that I am out of doors without my maid."

"Yes, I expect she would. Where are you headed?" Regina turned to look behind her. "Only two houses can be found at the end of this street, and I doubt you were bringing *me* a present."

Regina's brother, the Duke of Lennox, owned a modestly sized townhouse that dated back a hundred years. Miles was a mere lord, and yet his house could only be described as a mansion, bedecked with marble. It towered over the street, windows sparkling in the sunshine and roofed over with scalloped tiles, looking like an extravagant wedding cake.

He could certainly afford to keep his illegitimate children in comfort.

Daisy managed a smile. "I'm delivering a basket of fruit for Clementine. As I told you before, our families have long acquaintance. I often bring baked goods and such for the family."

"Your bodice is very low," Regina said, frowning. "Men might take that as an invitation, especially when a woman is as ... as bouffant as you are. A fichu would be a good addition. Would you like to borrow my maid? Just to make certain that you are not accosted?"

Rather surprisingly, Regina looked genuinely concerned.

"The street is empty," Daisy pointed out.

"I believe that Clementine has gone to Bath to see her sisters, so you definitely shouldn't enter the house unaccompanied."

"In that case, I shall merely hand this basket to a footman."

"I have decided to encourage Lord Devin's courtship," Lady Regina said musingly. "His birth and fortune are excellent. I like the idea of living next door to my brother and sister-in-law, even though Beatrice and I have had a few squabbles. The only drawback is that Lord Devin has a withering manner. But does that matter in a spouse?"

"He does seem to be frightfully ill-tempered," Daisy said. To her horror, she saw her fichu pop upwards, as if a little foot had kicked it from underneath. "I'm sure you can do better. It was lovely seeing you, Lady Regina." She slipped by. "If you'll excuse me, I must return home expeditiously."

She could feel Regina's gaze drilling into her all the way down the street, but she didn't look around, not even when she was climbing the marble steps leading to Number Forty-Nine, nor when Lord Devin's butler opened the door. He was an elderly man with coiffed hair that rivaled the color of his white shirt.

"Good morning, Miss," he said with ceremonious gravity.

"I am Miss Peacham," she announced. "I must see Lord Devin. Immediately."

The butler glanced over her shoulder, no doubt looking for a maid or chaperone.

"I have private business with his lordship."

His eyes narrowed.

"I shall attend him in his library," Daisy said, walking straight past the butler, because if her mother had taught her anything, it was how to cow a servant. "I suppose it's down the corridor?"

"Excuse me! Miss!"

She marched ahead, forcing the butler to follow her. He shuffled after her, just overtaking her in time to open a door and announce, "A young lady, my lord."

"For God's sake, Hobbs," Miles drawled from somewhere inside. "Take care of it yourself, won't you? I have to finish this report."

"That's *Miss Peacham* to you," Daisy snapped at Hobbs, getting into her role. She brushed past him again, walked into the room, and closed the door in the butler's face.

"Hello, Miles."

Episode 101:
Her Name is Belle?

Miles was seated at his desk, writing up a report for Lord Paget, the Lord High Steward. *"My investigation has proved that Lady Lamont had an amorous relationship with the household's third footman, as evidenced by several letters. The lady wrote those missives not realizing that the object of her affections was illiterate; the affair was discovered when the footman asked the cook to read them aloud."*

He put down his quill. Lord Lamont wanted a divorce; his lady just wanted the footman. When he first began working with Lord Paget, three years ago, he found such cases interesting. Now he felt besmirched by the sexual depravity that "polite" society ignored.

Not for the first time, he considered stepping away from his position in the House of Lords. He would be deeply grateful to return to a state of ignorance with regard to his peers.

Yesterday he had listened to a pained lady explain her husband's penchant for behavior so outrageous that she faltered in her explanation, bursting into tears. Thereafter, he interviewed a lord who insisted that it was his wife's clumsiness that had caused her to fall down the stairs; his father-in-law was entirely mistaken when he insisted that he—her husband—had pushed her. "I treat my wife like a queen," he had blustered, turning red in the face.

If Miles had ever believed in innocence and decency, he didn't any longer. Daisy's face flashed through his mind, and he pushed the image away.

He was doing his best to ignore her. Allow her to kiss her young suitors. Younger-than-he suitors. He had made up his mind to marry, but certainly not someone whose flirtatious ways inspired homicidal jealousy. Which is what he felt about her.

That would be madness.

His butler, Hobbs, opened the door and gobbled something, even though Miles had explicitly told the man that he was working.

"For God's sake, Hobbs," Miles said, taking up his quill. "Take care of it yourself, won't you? I have to finish this report."

"That's *Miss Peacham* to you," a lady's voice said—not just any voice. It was unmistakably Daisy's. He surged to his feet.

Sure enough, Daisy was closing the door in his butler's face.

"Hello, Miles."

Where in the hell was her chaperone? Lady Wharton would be appalled by this clandestine visit. The conversation they had following his first and only proposal of marriage had become one of his least favorite memories.

Lately he found himself waking at night and questioning his choices as a younger man. Yes, he had enjoyed the charms of opera dancers, though he'd never engaged in adulterous relationships, as did many of his peers. He had always used a condom and thankfully had avoided catching syphilis or another such disease.

Even so, his reputation had become a millstone around his neck, dragging him to the level of those he investigated.

As he walked toward the door, Daisy turned to him. Sparks of alarm went through him: her hair was more disarranged than normal, and her eyes were red. She'd been crying.

"What's the matter?" he asked sharply.

"Everything," she said. "Everything has gone wrong, Miles. I didn't know where else to turn." She glanced down.

He hadn't even noticed that she was carrying a basket, let alone a basket from which a small foot was waving in the air. His breath caught in his chest. "*Daisy.*"

Her mouth quivered into a shaky smile. "Daisy—and Belle."

Miles took the basket and pulled back the lace cover. The child took one look at him and let out a squeal that escalated into a shriek.

"Oh, my goodness," Daisy gasped, patting her shoulder. "Belle, please don't scream."

Not for nothing had Miles grown up with four younger sisters. He felt around to make sure the child was dry before he picked her up, dropping the basket to the floor. Somehow through a haze of disillusionment and fury, he managed to ask, "Her name is Belle?"

"Yes," Daisy said. "You are acquainted with babies, I see."

What right had *she* to narrow her eyes at him? She was the one carting around an infant who was her spitting image. An adorable baby. Even in the grip of sheer, bloody jealousy, he had to admit that.

"I am," he said coolly. "Not entirely willingly."

Why should he be surprised that she had a child? No one in polite society was exempt from the uncivilized behavior he saw every day—and that included young ladies. If anything, Daisy was more honest than most, since she had jested about her future husband's adultery. Moreover, she had attended that masquerade, so her innocence had always been in doubt.

"I am impressed," she said, somewhat surprisingly. "I find your readiness to admit familiarity with children to be honorable."

"Honor has nothing to do with it." After he and his elder sister were born, his parents had allowed a decade to pass before they had a sudden spate of offspring. When they died of influenza on the same terrible day, he stepped into parenthood at the age of fourteen.

The household had included nursemaids, a nanny, and a governess, but when a little girl shrieks so loudly for her brother that she can be heard two floors below? He'd climbed the stairs to the nursery over and over, because there had been no other choice.

"I gather the father of this child is not honorable," he said now.

"No, he is not." Daisy's plump lips thinned and pressed together.

"I'll kill him," Miles said calmly. Belle had been startled into silence when he picked her up. Now she leaned closer and patted his emerging beard curiously. Fearless. Just like her mother. "I will cut out his liver and leave it for crows to eat."

Daisy let out an odd sound, like a hiccup. "You can't do that."

The blackguard who fathered this child and deserted it, without marrying her mother, would face his naked blade—but Daisy didn't need to know of the details.

Belle popped her thumb in her mouth and started sucking with a vigor that suggested that she was hungry.

Which meant more screaming soon.

Where had the child been cared for since birth? Belle must have been wet nursed somewhere, because no gently born young lady could admit to having a child out of wedlock. Regardless, wherever this one had been, she had found her way back to Daisy.

Lady Wharton's rigid face drifted into his mind. He had a pretty good idea why Daisy had fled to his house: she had been thrown out. Most ladies of his acquaintance would be sobbing, begging for help, in hysterics. Daisy had clearly been crying, but she was dignified even in extremis.

"I need—I need your help, Miles."

"Surely the child's father would be a better candidate than I am?" Despite himself, his voice hardened. "I can ensure his support."

"My understanding is that he's happy to send the child to an orphanage."

Miles was boggled. A man had slept with Daisy and didn't want to marry her? Didn't want to legitimize his own child? Wanted to send *his own child* to an orphanage?

"What a hellhound," he growled.

Tears welled in Daisy's eyes.

"He's married, isn't he?"

She flinched. He saw the truth in her face. Daisy had been seduced by an adulterous rogue, quite likely an acquaintance. His hands felt hot, as if he had a fever, but he kept his voice even. "Were you forced, Daisy?" The words shot from his mouth like bullets.

"No!" she squeaked. "Nothing like that!"

He took a deep breath. Only one solution presented itself.

"I don't know what to do," Daisy cried. "If Belle is sent to an orphanage, I shall never see her again." A sob tore from her chest. "Belle might fall ill or even die, and I wouldn't know. I keep thinking that they might not keep her warm."

Miles's gut twisted at the abject misery in her face.

She drifted closer until he could smell her apple blossom fragrance. "I thought," she said, her voice shaking, "that perhaps you could add her to yours."

He frowned. "To mine?"

Belle let out a warning squeal. Miles glanced down and found the baby was giving him a guileless smile that said, "Feed me, if you please." She wasn't just an enchanting child; she seemed to have an even temperament.

"Yes. Wherever you keep them. Yours." Words tumbled from Daisy's lips. "I love the way you are holding her. I respect you for that, I truly do. The easy solution is to send a child to an orphanage. But that's not right. I suppose yours are in the country?"

Miles drew in a harsh breath. "*Mine*?" he rasped.

She nodded.

"You think that I have bastard children? More than one?" He had just been thinking about his reputation, but it seemed it was worse than he imagined.

Daisy's eyes were exhausted, red . . . surprised. "Don't you?"

Episode 102:
No Nest for This Cuckoo

"I have no bastards," Miles said bitingly. "I have *no children*, born within wedlock or without."

Daisy blinked at him. His reputation was unearned. But she'd seen him…

"You think that I have a fistful of bastards off in the country, and you hoped to hide this child among the rest, a cuckoo in the nest?"

"Yes," she said baldly.

Miles was clearly furious, his body rigid. "I'm sorry to disappoint you, but my sins are not sufficient enough to camouflage yours." The veneer of a politic, sophisticated gentleman had been stripped away. He looked like a Pict warrior she had seen depicted in a history book. Blue slashes of paint on his cheekbones would hardly make him look any more ferocious.

Daisy swallowed hard. This was a disaster. If he had no place to put Belle, then he could not help. If she told him that Belle was her half-sister, he would go straight to the Albany and accost her father—which would result in Belle being put in an orphanage. She would be gone forever, and Daisy would never see her again.

The baby pulled her thumb out of her mouth and frowned, as if she too was insulted. In one deft movement, Miles swung her over his head, flying her around as if she were an ungainly bird.

Daisy started forward, fearful he would drop her, but Belle began giggling and broke into a peal of laughter, kicking up her legs in delight. Miles's entire face transformed as he smiled at the child.

He may not have any children, but he would be a marvelous father someday. He lowered Belle and tucked her into the crook of his arm.

"She'll last two minutes at most," Miles said. As he turned to Daisy, his laughing eyes lost all expression. "I suggest we dispatch her to the kitchen while we discuss the situation."

The baby caught the corner of Miles's neckcloth and began chewing on it busily.

"Ew, what on earth is she doing?" Daisy cried.

He pulled his cravat away, and Belle promptly replaced it with her thumb. "She's teething. Your mothering skills seem somewhat lacking. Where has Belle been living while you were circling the ballroom floor?"

Daisy's mind reeled at this rude—albeit fair—observation. "That's none of your business!" she said hotly. "How do you know so much about children?"

"*Not* due to bastard children. I have younger sisters, and my parents passed away when they were very little."

She should have gone to Frederick. Miles had looked at her with indifference before this morning, but now his eyes held pure contempt.

It enraged her at a basic level. He had gone to that masquerade. What right had he to be so holier-than-thou, even if he didn't have such children? Not that she had one, but if she did…Her thoughts got tangled up in the unfairness. The only conclusion was that the world was unfair—but most keenly unfair to children like Belle and women like Belle's mother.

"Forgive me for intruding. We shall leave," she said.

"And go where?" Miles bounced Belle gently. She stopped sucking her thumb, patted his face again, and opined "Moo."

Miles raised an eyebrow. "Are her greetings limited to bovine imitations?"

"It's a nice sound," Daisy said defensively. "Give her to me, if you please."
"No."

It was incredibly seductive watching Miles cuddle a baby so tenderly, perhaps because she'd never seen a man do anything of the sort. Then his refusal filtered into her mind.

"What do you mean, *no*?" she asked sharply.

"I gather your mother threw you out?"

"Actually, I left," Daisy said. But when she opened her mouth to explain, he interrupted.

"This child is hungry, and you appear unprepared to care for her, as you have no nappies or appropriate food. I suggest that you don't leave the house in the future without carrying rusks. My sisters had to be fed at odd hours."

Daisy accepted that reprimand as fair enough, so she nodded. "I shall learn to care for her." Surprisingly, given that she had originally thought to send Belle to the country, she meant it.

Watching Belle smiling at someone else made her feel peculiar. She didn't want Belle to grow up with another woman.

Belle was *hers*.

His eyes narrowed. "Do you even know what a rusk is?"

"Of course I do!" Regina had frequently suggested that Daisy eat nothing but rusks in order to whittle down her hips. "If you have some in the kitchens, I shall give her one and we can take our leave."

"And go where?"

"To Frederick," she snapped.

His face grew—if possible—even more rigid. "I should have known. Although I would have thought that Frederick's penchant for whiskey might have affected his ability to father a child. And he is not married, by the way."

Daisy wasn't entirely sure what he was talking about, but her friend obviously needed defending. "How dare you!" she cried. "Frederick can do ... can do whatever he wishes!"

"Obviously." Miles visibly struggled for control. "Let's hope he is sober enough to manage a rapier."

"What are you talking about?"

"He deserted this child. He deserted *you*. I had no idea that when you were working so cozily together on your uncle's letters he was seducing you. I would have—"

"Done what?" Daisy asked wildly. "Frederick wasn't seducing me!"

"So you seduced him?" A vein was pulsing in Miles's forehead. "I would be grateful to be spared the distasteful series of events that resulted in this child."

"Belle is *not* Frederick's child!"

A prickly silence fell between them.

Miles's brows drew together. "So are you planning to beg Frederick for help, just as you did me? If he is the man I take him for, he has no bastards, Daisy. And not because of whiskey. I lost my temper and shouldn't have said that."

"That is none of your business," Daisy stated.

"You came to me. You *made* it my business."

"That's when I thought—" She broke off.

"When you thought that I had a schoolroom full of bastards?" He snorted. "I suppose your mother informed you that I was a rakehell. I assure you that my reputation has been blown out of proportion. Surely you didn't think that you could simply drop this child on my doorstep and return to society as if nothing had occurred, as if Belle didn't exist?" Miles's eyes darkened with distaste, but his voice remained even.

Daisy swallowed hard, since that had been precisely what she'd envisioned.

"This child makes you ineligible for marriage in polite society," Miles stated.

Daisy instantly knew that she was hearing the cool distance with which Miles addressed miscreants in the House of Lords. People like her uncle.

"Surely you understand," he continued, "that you cannot simply return to the ballroom as if nothing happened, as if you had never given birth. Although I gather that's precisely what you have been doing since the Season opened."

Daisy felt a blinding wave of fury. "You need not be so condescending," she retorted, her voice cracking. It would probably take practice to sound as calmly patronizing as he.

"I am being practical. I spend my days investigating sexual depravity amongst the nobility," Miles said with scathing emphasis. "I am surprised that Lady Wharton had the gall to bring you to the marriage market this fall knowing that you birthed a child. I assure you that such dishonesty is no basis for marriage."

"Marriage?" Daisy repeated. "Marriage to whom?"

"To a husband whom you entranced *without telling the truth*. What about your wedding night? Virginity is highly valued. I've always known you were impulsive, Daisy, but this sort of behavior is a new low."

How could she ever have imagined they were friends?

"Unfortunately your free-spirited ideas are not shared by most gentlemen in polite society. I will say in your favor that you have never pretended to be sanctimonious."

Daisy couldn't believe that she'd ever had an infatuation with the pompous, arrogant arse who was standing before her. He sounded as if he was a solicitor, doling out charges at the bar.

"Did you consider what would happen after your husband discovered that not only were you unchaste, but that you had given birth?" he demanded. "The event leaves marks on a woman's body, as I'm sure you are aware."

Daisy had no idea what the marks might be, but that was irrelevant. "You are outrageous ... horrible!" she spluttered.

"If you had been party to the cases I have investigated, you would be as cynical as I. *Polite* society is nothing more than a cesspool of sexual profligacy."

"Amongst your friends, perhaps," she said scathingly. "Fellows like Rothingale, who entertain you one minute and try to seduce your sister the next. Can there be anything worse than a man who chides a lady for not wearing a halo—when he himself pranced around a masquerade looking for a mistress?"

Miles's face shut like a trap. "An error on my part. Your mother kindly pointed out my transgressions. As for the halo, evidence suggests that your claims for that—or a white veil—were lost some time ago."

She was so angry that she couldn't even think straight. "What do you know of women's bodies? Men are fools in that respect, as in so many others. I shall leave and you can forget all about me and my sexual—what was the term? Profligacy?"

His jaw clenched. "I should not have spoken so, and I was not referring to you. Obviously a man took advantage of you. *He* is the cesspool."

Daisy snorted. "There is no cesspool in my life."

Then she winced, remembering her father.

His eyes caught the gesture and softened. "There's only one solution to your problem, Daisy, and we both know it."

"I will not allow Belle to be sent to an orphanage!" She took in a deep breath. "If you're going to suggest that she be housed in the country, I refuse that as well." She reached out her arms, and Belle leaned toward her, making Daisy's heart burst with tenderness. "I intend to raise her myself, no matter the scandal," she said, snuggling Belle against her breast.

"In that case, I'll marry you."

She gaped at him. "What?"

"We'll marry by special license." Miles's voice was even. He no longer looked contemptuous but resigned. "What did you think would happen when you came here?"

"Not that. I thought you had—"

His hand slashed through the air. "Nonsense! You brought that child to me knowing that I would have to marry you."

"I didn't," Daisy gasped. "Given your reputation, I thought this was a problem you had faced before. I wouldn't marry *you* if you were the last man in the world!"

He laughed. "Are you quite certain?"

She felt her face turning red with embarrassment. "Marry *you*?" She was proud of her sarcastic tone. "I came to you because of your reputation. I wouldn't want to marry a man whose morals are so loose!"

It was a lie. Even now, with the way he was looking at her, with the assumptions he made about her, she only had to look at him to feel a wash of longing.

"There's only one solution, Daisy, and it's marriage."

Behind him, the door to the library opened.

Hobbs entered and announced, "The Lady Regina."

Glimpsing the baby in Daisy's arms, the butler's eyes widened. Regina shoved him to the side and traipsed into the room, followed by her maid.

"I've grown concerned about the reputation of my dear friend, Miss Wharton," she said brightly. "I know that..." Her voice faltered into silence. With a sharp jerk, she slammed the door in Hobb's face.

Belle lifted her head and smiled at the new arrival. "Moo!"

Episode 103:
A Scene of Debauchery

Slashes of crimson colored Regina's cheeks. "Miss Wharton!" she gasped. "You—you—and Lord Devin—"

Daisy panicked. Desperation churned in her gut. To this point she'd lied by omission, but now... "It is *not* his baby!" she cried. "It is *my* baby!"

Miles didn't respond, but Regina curled her lip.

"My child," Daisy repeated, her voice croaking.

Regina fixed her with a basilisk's glare. "Obviously. The resemblance is unmistakable. I am appalled that you disguised your debauched relationship by pretending that you and Lord Devin were merely old friends."

"I had not anticipated a morning call from you, Lady Regina," Miles said.

"And I thought you, Lord Devin, to be an honorable gentleman, despite your tawdry reputation," Regina retorted. "It is salutary to know the truth. This situation is remarkably distasteful. I feel tarnished by proximity. My mother will be horrified."

She showed no sign of taking her outraged self out the door, though.

As if on cue, Belle let out a high screech that made Daisy jump.

"Young woman," Miles said to Regina's maid, "take this child downstairs and ask the cook to feed her some porridge." A vein was throbbing in his forehead.

After a nod from Regina, the woman walked out of the room, holding Belle at arm's length as if she were a cat fished from a rain barrel.

"Please don't let us keep you, Lady Regina," Miles said with biting emphasis, "since you feel so… What *do* you feel? How precisely do you think that standing in this room will tarnish your person?"

"I rang the bell out of Christian charity, worried that Miss Wharton's reputation would be dented by spending time under your roof without a chaperone," Regina said righteously. "Had I known that I was entering a scene of debauchery, I would have stayed far away."

"I congratulate you on your benevolent instincts," Miles replied. "However, I'm afraid that you are *de trop*. Miss Wharton and I are in the midst of a significant discussion."

"I imagine that you are," Regina said, looking as if her feet were glued to the floor. "*Very* significant. That child is clearly yours, Lord Devin. It has its mother's eyes and its father's bone structure."

Daisy opened her mouth, but Miles glanced at her and snarled, "No." Then he turned to Regina. "I would like you to leave. No explanation is owed to you, nor shall any be given."

Regina sniffed. Her face had settled into lines of heavy disapproval, making her look several decades older than she was. "That child is some months old, which suggests that *you*, Miss Wharton, formed an alliance with Lord Devin sometime last year, presumably after you were absent from polite society due to your uncle's misdemeanors or while in mourning for his death. To think that I was considering taking *you*, Lord Devin, for a husband. I was close to accepting your hand."

Perhaps Regina expected Miles to look dismayed? Daisy fancied she could see thunderclouds forming around his head.

"I was not aware that I was being considered for such an honor," he said with searing directness. "Your consideration does not align with my inclinations. I had no intention of proposing to you."

A ringing silence filled the room.

Regina had been red with indignation; now she paled, blinking rapidly.

"You shouldn't make any rash judgments, Lord Devin," Daisy said impulsively. "Lady Regina was shocked by the presence of a baby."

"I wouldn't take your leavings, Miss Wharton," Regina said, regaining some of her fire.

Miles turned to Daisy. "*Really*? Are you encouraging me to propose to Lady Regina?"

Another terrible silence.

"No," she whispered.

"Excellent," Miles said. "Since you're marrying me, it would have been most disconcerting to have you foisting me onto another woman."

"He has despoiled your innocence," Regina spat. "I blame Lady Wharton for the scanty nature of your bodices, which necessarily drew male lust. I fear that society will not take this news well."

"Lord Devin didn't know of the baby until today," Daisy said, trying desperately to think of a way out of the morass without bringing shame to her mother.

"Some will excuse him on those grounds," Regina said. "I shall ever fault him for his ungentlemanly behavior in seducing you in the first place, low bodices or no!"

"I will have to live with your opinion," Miles said grimly. His eyes weren't contemptuous. They were blank. Void of any feeling.

Daisy took a deep breath. Her mind was whirling, and she could scarcely think. The conversation was moving so quickly that it felt out of her control. Guilt gnawed at her stomach. Miles didn't want to marry her—he didn't even like her—but now he had announced their marriage to Regina, of all people.

"If you, Lord Devin, had married Miss Wharton before the child was born, the situation might have been salvaged," Regina said, a near-gleeful tone in her voice. "Your reputation, such as it is, will be *ruined*. My brother will be gravely disappointed in you. I shall write him at once."

Miles's eyes flared. "I don't give a damn what you will or won't do. I'm marrying Daisy, but my decision has nothing to do with you. If you would please return to your own domicile, Lady Regina, I intend to arrange for an immediate marriage."

"My brother considers you his closest friend but even he will never forgive you." She laughed shrilly. "I doubt that Lord Paget will wish for *you* to continue investigating the crimes of the aristocracy. The fox minding the henhouse!"

Horror went down Daisy's spine. It was one thing to ruin her own reputation, although she couldn't bear to think about her mother at the moment. But Miles's as well? If it hadn't been for the stupid impulse that sent her to his house begging for help, he wouldn't be obligated to marry her.

"Regina, if you tell *anyone* about Belle, I shall describe precisely what happened when you accosted my cousin's husband, Major FitzRoy, last year," she blurted out.

Regina opened her mouth, but Daisy raised a finger. "Society has been allowed to think that you jilted Major FitzRoy, causing him to turn to my cousin Livie. That will no longer be the case. Frederick will confirm my account."

For a moment she thought that Regina would be unable to contain herself, but then a mask of civility fell over her face, only her eyes showing her stark rage. "I fail to see how my silence will help your situation, but I shall certainly hold my tongue."

"You will not only remain silent, but you will actively support our marriage," Miles said. "In six months, society will be notified that one of my wife's distant relatives recently died in India, orphaning a child."

Regina looked as stunned as Daisy felt. "India?"

"Haven't either of you noticed the preponderance of children who are supposedly orphaned and sent home from that country?"

Daisy shook her head.

"How distasteful," Regina said.

"It's the child's only chance at a respectable future. When the time comes, she will debut with an extravagant dowry, supposedly the inheritance from her father's work for the East India Trading Company. We will tactfully acknowledge that the child's *father* was illegitimate, which is why he doesn't appear in Debrett's, but *she* is the orphaned daughter of a wholesome marriage."

"I had no idea you were so imaginative," Daisy said, stunned.

"I am not imaginative," Miles said. "I am merely well-acquainted with the sins of the aristocracy. We will marry tomorrow in the Duke of Lennox's private chapel, which will allow Lady Regina to spread the news that we are desperately in love."

"I will?" Regina asked.

The look on his face made her fall back a step. "I suppose I could do that."

"I will send footmen out to invite a select few to the ceremony tomorrow," Miles continued. "You, Lady Regina, will cheerfully attest to nurturing our romance. Your enthusiasm for our love story—and the fact we are marrying in your family's chapel—will quell the *pity* you would otherwise receive."

Peevishness was replaced by horror as Regina's eyes rounded. "Pity?"

"As yet another prospective bridegroom turns away," Miles said pointedly.

Regina's eyelashes fluttered but she recovered quickly. "You certainly can't do a wedding breakfast here, given your ancient butler, so I shall host the event following the ceremony."

Daisy felt paralyzed. Her life had begun unraveling at the seams that morning, and now it was reshaping without her input. "That would be very kind of you, Regina," she managed.

"Yes, it would," Regina said petulantly. "After all, I had quite decided to marry you myself, Lord Devin."

Miles groaned. "Must we—"

Regina cut him off. "If you wish to persuade society that your marriage is a case of love and not scandal, you should keep all polite observances. Lady Wharton's feelings are quite likely disarranged, so I shall do this from the goodness of my heart."

She flounced from the room without another word.

"Goodness of her heart *my ass!*" Miles snarled.

Episode 104:
It Could Have Been Worse

Pinpricks needled down her body as Daisy forced herself to turn and meet Miles's eyes. She felt swamped by guilt and horror. "I'm so sorry!" she all but wailed. "I had no idea that Regina would follow me to your house."

Miles's cheekbones were drawn tight, his eyes dark as pitch. "That woman is a harpy."

Daisy felt a tear slide down her cheek. "I've ruined you," she whispered. "Forced you to marry me in order to protect me, when Belle isn't yours. I've *ruined* you."

"I do not consider myself ruined," Miles said, "though I'll admit that my future just took a sharp right turn. Damn it, Daisy, what in the hell are you doing, bringing your child here? No, forget that," he muttered. "Too late."

"I wasn't thinking clearly!" Daisy cried. "It was … It was an impulse. A foolish impulse."

"I have one question: Who is the father? I'm going to give myself the pleasure of slaying him on the way to Doctors' Commons to acquire a special license."

Daisy took one look at his murderous expression and knew that her father's life was in her hands.

"I can't tell you that," she gulped.

"You *must* tell me," Miles snarled. "I'm raising this man's bastard, and I'm giving the lass a handsome dowry. I deserve that information."

"No!" Daisy cried. She dashed away another tear.

He took a step closer, his expression forbidding. "Do you know what makes a marriage successful?"

Daisy shook her head. Clearly, her parents had not provided a role model.

"Honesty between husband and wife. Honesty and loyalty. *Not* loyalty to previous lovers."

"I am not loyal to him," Daisy promised with a fervency in her voice that she hoped sounded convincing. "Please, could we start over?"

"Start over from the moment when you strolled into my house, basket in hand? I wish that was possible. Where is your father in all this, by the way? I presume Lord Wharton knows of that child?"

"He doesn't," Daisy said, pretty sure that was true. "He has no idea. He doesn't live with us."

"I've heard as much."

"My father lives in a bachelor apartment in the Albany." Another tear slid down her cheek. In a lifetime of impulsive misdeeds, walking to Miles's house had to be her worst—and that included sneaking into Rothingale's masquerade. She had practically invited Lady Regina to conclude that Miles was a dastardly rake who would seduce a young lady.

"Given the knowledge I've gained in the House of Lords, I might as well accept that every young lady on the marriage market has entertained several lovers before she appears at her debut ball, swathed in virginal white, some months later trotting up the altar trailing a veil," Miles said grimly.

"I'm sure that's not the case," Daisy said uncertainly.

Miles shook his head. Misery and exhaustion were etched on his future wife's face, yet her cheeks held a rosy flush, and her gaze was pure and clear beneath welling tears. How could she look so innocent?

Yes, she was impulsive in visiting him. But she came to ask him for help.

He had to admit that he liked that.

The idea of Daisy wandering the city with a baby in a basket was abhorrent. In fact, when he next saw Lady Wharton—presumably at the wedding—he would say as much. What was she thinking, throwing her daughter into the street?

He'd never liked the woman, but he had respected her moral sense. When she attacked his reputation, he had accepted the judgment as deserving. But now, he decided broodingly, Lady Wharton was very, very lucky that he was marrying her daughter, because otherwise he would have told all of London just what a hypocrite she was.

"I'm so sorry," Daisy rasped. "I know you don't want to marry me."

"It could be worse," he replied. "I could have been forced to marry Lady Regina. *She* would likely cause a fuss at being immured in the country."

"What?"

"You and Belle will have to stay in the country for a few months until we can announce the demise of family. I don't think that either of us are good enough actors to carry off true love on close examination, do you?"

Daisy's eyes filled with tears again.

Miles felt a bolt of guilt. Damn it, he felt as if he were bullying her. He had an irrational urge to take his fiancée into his arms and comfort her.

He'd never been fool enough to imagine his marriage as a great love affair. At least he knew that his future wife was fertile. Was that too cynical?

"I should return home and speak to my mother," Daisy said. Her silvery hair had fallen from its pins and was spilling down over her shoulders. Her snub nose was red.

The urge to comfort her turned to an ache, so he drew Daisy across the room and sat down, pulling her onto his lap. It felt absurdly right when she curled against his shoulder.

"Don't worry," Miles said, aware that Daisy was having the precise effect on him offered by so-called aphrodisiacs. Her hair smelled like apple blossoms and sunshine. He'd always scoffed at the idea that a medical drug could invigorate a man's desire ... but if you bottled that perfume?

He wound his arms around her, aware that his tool was thickening under her arse. No need to worry about whether he would shock her. No wonder she had leaned back against him at the ball; she *knew* how a woman pleasures a man. Remembering that moment sent more sensual hunger surging through his body.

"Sorry," he muttered.

"What are you apologizing for? I'm the one..." Daisy's chin quivered as she looked up at him. "I'm the one who came to you as if I were a homing pigeon. Except I was a pigeon bringing the plague because now you have to marry me, and you don't want to, and you'll have to dowry Belle, and—"

"You did not bring the plague," Miles interrupted, registering that his voice had dropped into a husky tone that he only used in the bedroom.

"You're angry. *Justly* angry," she gulped. More tears slide down her cheeks.

He tightened his embrace. "I was angry, but now I'm getting used to the idea. After all, I had already decided to take a wife. Why not you? You get along with Clementine. I'm sure my other sisters will love you."

She huddled a little closer, only one wet cheek visible.

"You'll do."

It occurred to him that "You'll do" wasn't exactly romantic.

"You're beautiful. And experienced," he added with sudden energy. "Why would a man want to bed a lady who knows nothing in bed? It must be tedious. Boring. Painful for her, I understand. Was it painful for you?"

"Was what painful for me?" Daisy asked, wiping away more tears.

She probably thought he was talking about giving birth. His mind instinctively veered away from the fact that she had given birth to another man's child.

Miles handed her his handkerchief. "Nothing important. My point was that I do well to marry you." Satisfaction spread through him, the kind of feeling a man has after he endows an orphanage. He was doing the right thing, the kindly thing. "It will save your reputation and allow Belle to be introduced to society."

He kissed the top of her silky head. "We will have an excellent marriage." The words rumbled in his chest like a promise.

"Perhaps," Daisy said, shaking out his handkerchief. She didn't sound as convinced as he was. "Didn't you hope to fall in love before you agreed to marry?"

"No," Miles said without hesitation. "I've never been in love. It looks like a very uncomfortable state, not to mention temporary."

Daisy sighed. "I think you know this already, but I might as well admit that I'm in love with you."

At first Miles thought he hadn't heard her correctly. But as the words sunk in, he realized that if she was in love with *him*, she couldn't be in love with the baby's father.

That was excellent.

He cleared his throat, trying to think how to respond. "I'm honored by your affection," he said, knowing he sounded like an awkward ass.

Daisy pushed a cloud of hair away from her eyes. "Don't worry. I understand that you don't feel the same. It's been terribly uncomfortable, so hopefully it *is* temporary. Ever since the evening when my gown fell to the floor, I can't stop looking for you everywhere." She blew her nose and then added, "It's been so humiliating. At least when we're married, I'll know where you are."

She gave him a watery smile. "I'm sure I'll quickly grow tired of having you around."

Miles generally looked for her as well, but only because Daisy was so much more interesting than the other young women he was courting. Not that he had been courting her. But he had kept an eye on her, just in case she experienced another problem with her clothing.

"In fact, once we're married, I expect the feeling will quickly wane," she continued, sounding slightly more cheerful. "I don't know any married couples who voluntarily spend time together, other than my cousin Livie and her husband."

"My best friend Jonah and his wife Bea," Miles put in. "He scarcely comes to London now that they have a son, William."

"Will you mind living in the country?"

"I'll return to the city after a week. I have a number of cases coming up to trial in the House of Lords."

"You can't," Daisy said, straightening. "We are supposed to be desperately in love, remember? Major FitzRoy took Livie with him to *war*. A besotted man wouldn't leave his bride after a mere week."

Her bottom was maddeningly lush, so Miles was having trouble keeping his mind on the conversation. "Besotted," he repeated.

"That means people have to believe that *you* are in love with me, just as I am with you."

"A week isn't good enough?" Miles shifted his legs, thinking of how much he wanted to carry her upstairs to his bedchamber. In fact, now he thought of it, seven days may not be long enough to sate himself. "I could stay longer on the estate," he offered. "I could..."

He could tell Lord Paget that he didn't want to investigate any more crimes. The idea felt like a glass of cold water on a blisteringly hot day.

"I could stay at least a month," he decided.

"Excellent," Daisy said, huddling back against his chest.

He was starting to feel quite content. Really, this was an excellent solution. Marrying Daisy meant having her in his bed, night after night.

Every night.

What's more, he liked Belle. She was a cheerful scrap of humanity, and he would be happy to father her.

He brushed the hair back from Daisy's cheek. "Feeling better?"

"More or less."

"We share something far more important than temporary infatuation," he said, making no attempt to hide the heat in his gaze.

She glanced up at him. "Oh?" Her eyelids flickered, and the corner of her lush mouth curled up.

Taking that as an invitation, Miles bent his head and licked into her mouth, her taste instantly igniting his body. He arrowed his fingers into her silky, messy curls so he could kiss her more deeply.

Daisy curled an arm around his neck, kissing him back. He could feel her nipples through her light gown, through his linen shirt, as her breasts pressed against his chest. A deep groan caught in his throat.

"Do I feel dazed because I'm in love with you, or because you kiss so much better than my other suitors?" she whispered after he pulled away just enough to breathe.

He registered the fact that Belle's father was apparently as unskilled in bed as he was worthless, but pushed the thought away. "We should stop," he managed sometime later, fighting the fact that his blood was on fire.

Daisy's eyes were still swollen, but she looked far happier. "I have one requirement for our marriage. I didn't think of it until now, but it's important."

Miles had the sudden realization that he didn't want her to fall out of love with him. He wanted her to be happy. "Yes?"

"No more Rothingale. No mistresses. No affairs with Russian dancers."

He traced her generous lower lip with one finger. "Are you saying that you and I will cleave unto each other—to use the Biblical phrase—til death do us part?"

Daisy took a deep breath. "Yes."

"No more kissing other men." The words jumped from his mouth without conscious volition. "Your very last impulsive act, as far as the male sex is concerned, was walking to my house."

Her lips curved. "I promise. No kissing anyone except my husband. The same for you."

Fidelity was obviously a worthy goal.

More to the point, Miles hadn't desired anyone since...He realized with a shock that he hadn't looked at a woman lustfully since the Rothingale masquerade. Not that it had anything to do with Daisy.

"I haven't had a mistress or a lover in some years," he told her. "I have a feeling that you, Lady Devin, will keep me busy."

Her laugh was not *bawdy*, precisely. It was joyful. The fact that his blood raced with pure lust at the sound?

Inexplicable.

Episode 105: The Prospect of Marital Intimacy

Down in the kitchens, Belle greeted them with cheerful "Moo," but showed no interest in leaving the maid who was feeding her mashed apple. Daisy was struck by an aching wish for Belle to beam at her and hold out her arms. The feeling confirmed that she was right to marry Miles, because that was the only way she could become Belle's mother.

"The child should remain below stairs so that she's not seen," her future husband said. "She will follow us to the country in a carriage with its curtains drawn."

Daisy couldn't help thinking that he was terribly dictatorial. In the normal course of a marriage—if he had fallen in love with her—she might have been able to stand her ground and tell him that she'd like Belle to travel in their carriage. But now?

She nodded.

Then she walked home accompanied by a footman, since Miles exhibited a disconcerting ferocity at the idea she might walk a few London streets without an escort.

The moment she entered her house, her mother tore out of the front parlor.

"Where have you been?" Lady Wharton cried. "I thought you had left forever, taking the baby with you!" Her eyes were feverishly bright, the skin drawn tight over her cheekbones.

"I didn't go far," Daisy said soothingly, drawing her mother back into the parlor. "Do let's sit down."

"Where's the baby? Where's Belle?" Her mother collapsed into a chair, her thin hands twisting together. "I can't stop thinking of the way you looked at me with abhorrence. I suddenly realized that I had sent those waifs to the orphanage without ever checking to see what happened to them."

"I didn't mean to look at *you* unkindly!" Daisy cried. "When I heard of Father's despicable behavior, I thought of *him* with abhorrence. My half-siblings are not your relatives. You made certain they were cared for and taught to support themselves. No one could expect more from you."

"*I* should have expected more from me," Lady Wharton said. "Wallowing in anger as I did...Why do I bother going to church on Sundays, if I can't be truly charitable? The fact that Belle has her own name, your curls, and a blanket just like yours made my mean-spiritedness all too clear." Her voice caught. "Where is she?"

"She is with Lord Devin," Daisy said. "Miles and I will marry and raise Belle together."

"*What?*"

"We will wed tomorrow morning by special license, spend the night in London, and then travel to the country the following day. Miles is sending footmen all over London with invitations."

"When the news about Belle spreads, everyone will think that the two of you had child out of wedlock," her mother said hollowly.

"Miles assures me that his household staff will not gossip about Belle's presence. In six months, he will announce that one of my father's cousins, born on the wrong side of the blanket, has sadly succumbed to a fever in India that also took his wife. My husband and I will be able to care for Belle under the guide of raising my uncle's orphaned child. In time, Belle will be introduced to society with a magnificent dowry supposedly left to her by her entrepreneurial father."

"Oh," Lady Wharton said faintly. "Oh, my goodness."

"Apparently many children orphaned abroad are actually illegitimate offspring of nobility." Daisy hesitated and admitted, "Miles thinks that Belle is my child."

Her mother's lips fell open as an expression of pure horror crossed her face. "Daisy! Your fiancée believes you are a fallen woman?"

Daisy nodded, feeling a pulse of guilt.

"Virginity remains the cornerstone of all marriages in the aristocracy. Every man wants—rightly or wrongly—to feel that his wife is his alone."

"Then he'll be happy to learn the truth!"

"You cannot lie to the man you're going to marry!" Lady Wharton's eyes widened. "Who does he think the father is?"

"I refused to tell him."

Her mother's expression was extremely pained. She cleared her throat. "I believe now is the time to share some details about marital intimacy."

"I know them," Daisy assured her. "I shall tell him the truth after our wedding. He'll be pleased to discover that I'm as pure as the driven snow." Despite herself, a sardonic note underlaid that sentence. For the life of her, she couldn't understand why a gentleman was free to take more than one mistress and yet insist on marrying an innocent lass. It wasn't fair.

"Actually, I doubt Lord Devin will be pleased," her mother stated. "No one likes to be lied to, Daisy, let alone married under false pretenses."

"It's only one lie," Daisy said, her stomach clenching into a knot. "Well, two lies. One about me and one about Belle."

Lady Wharton shook her head. "Please tell him now. Waiting until the wedding night is a recipe for disaster."

"I can't," Daisy said flatly. "Miles is marrying me to save my reputation. If he discovers that Belle isn't mine, he'll pivot to ensuring that Father accepts his responsibilities. Belle will be sent to the orphanage, and I'll never see her again."

"Not necessarily," her mother said. "You could volunteer at the Chelsea Orphanage. I've half a mind to join the board myself."

"Belle will not grow up in an orphanage," Daisy stated. "Miles didn't flinch at the idea of raising my illegitimate baby—nor dowering her. Who other than he would have so much forbearance? What gentleman can you imagine accepting—and cherishing—another man's child as his own?"

"It is true that Lord Devin proposed to you some time ago," her mother said, speculation in her eyes. "Perhaps he is infatuated."

"No."

"You can't be certain. He's far more refined than the lads courting you. He would never write you silly sonnets or send bunches of violets."

Violets were Daisy's favorite flower; she blinked away the thought that she would *love* a bunch from Miles. "Unfortunately for that rosy idea, he lectured me about the evils of falsely pretending to innocence and blathered on about cheating my future husband by passing myself off as a virgin. He was forced to marry me after Lady Regina entered the room."

Her mother gave a shriek. "Tell me it isn't so!"

"She has promised to hold her tongue," Daisy said. "My point is that I can't fool myself into thinking Miles is marrying me by his own inclination."

"I suppose not." Lady Wharton sighed. "You truly intend to *mother* this child?"

Daisy sprang up and then sank onto her knees by her mother's chair, taking her hands. "I was so lucky to have you as a mother—and so was Livie. You loved and cared for both of us, even though Livie is not related to you by blood. If I can be half the mother to Belle that you have been to Livie, she will be a very lucky little girl."

"I *never* cry," Lady Wharton declared, her tear-filled eyes belying the claim as she squeezed Daisy's hands in hers. She frowned and said in a crackling voice, "Your hair has fallen down again."

"Belle has my unruly curls. Perhaps you can train her to be neater than I am. Grandmothers have notable authority."

"I love you, Daisy. You do know that, don't you?"

"How could I not?" She got to her feet and leaned down to kiss her mother's cheek.

"I mean to find your father's children," Lady Wharton said heavily. "This morning, after you left, I instructed Tangle to locate them. I should never have weighed my reputation against those young lives."

"I know just what to do with them," Daisy exclaimed.

"You do?"

"That 'relative' of ours in India? He had a large family. We're not even sure how many, since he was estranged from my father. His eldest daughter is my age and was brought up in England. After his and his lady's untimely demise, Miles—Lord Devin—was named as the guardian to all of them."

"Given that at least one is your age, people are more likely to believe the story," her mother said thoughtfully. "You couldn't have given birth to your twin, no matter how similar you are in appearance—and in my memory, the first child left on our doorstep looked exactly like my own baby."

"I can't wait to meet her," Daisy said. "I shall introduce her to society next year!"

"She may be a charwoman," her mother pointed out. "I've always thought of you as fearless, but even for you, that suggestion is mad."

"Mad, but just?"

"Don't speak to me of righteousness when you're beginning your marriage with falsehoods," her mother said tartly. "Just when do you plan to inform your new husband that not only is Belle your half-sibling, but that you intend to adopt four or five more?"

"I'll share my virginity on our wedding night," Daisy said, giving her mother an impish smile. "That will make him cheerful, given the absurd weight that men give to that foolishness. I'll save Belle's brothers and sisters for the next morning over breakfast."

Her mother began laughing. "Where did you come from, Daisy? Where did you get your fearlessness?"

"From you," Daisy said, holding out her hand. "Will you please come upstairs and help me choose a wedding costume? I am thinking of walking to the altar in the pillar of salt."

"The what?"

"My Egyptian mummy gown. It's so very white. The whitest white gown I have."

"You needn't wear white! Princess Charlotte's gown was a lovely cream silk with metallic lace."

"Miles made some ill-advised comments about strumpets disguising themselves in white. I have to live up to his expectations of a hussy."

"But you are a maiden!" her mother cried.

Daisy grinned. "Not for long."

"*Daisy!*"

Episode 106: Once Declared Man and Wife...

A few months ago, just after the archbishop declared Major FitzRoy and Livie "man and wife," Livie's new husband had caught up his wife at the altar and given her an utterly delightful, utterly scandalous kiss.

Daisy had mopped up tears at the sheer romance of watching Livie's silk gown billowing in the air due to the tightness of her new husband's embrace. Even her mother had grown dewy-eyed.

Her wedding was clearly not going to inspire any romantic tears.

For one thing, Daisy's fiancé was nowhere to be seen, though the ceremony had been due to begin some twenty minutes ago.

"The bride is supposed to be late, not the groom," Regina hissed on her way to greet a newly arrived guest. "Do you suppose he's run off to the colonies?"

Daisy managed a weak smile. She believed in Miles. Counted on him. Surely he would arrive. From the corner of her eye, she could see guests whispering to each other.

As the minutes ticked by, she felt as if little fault lines were forming in her heart. The ducal chapel echoed with chattering voices, but they seemed to come from a distance. With nothing else to do, Daisy kept smiling, her heartbeat fluctuating every time the door opened.

"Are you sure about this?" Frederick asked, drifting up to her. "My offer's still open. I don't have as much money, but despite my hangover, I got here on time. I'd be proud to walk the aisle with you, even given that dress. You couldn't find another rag to throw on?"

"I look regal," Daisy told him, unoffended.

"I'd say divine," Frederick said. He gave her a crooked smile. "As well as very pretty and approachable. You make me wish that I'd done better at courting you, Daisy. Convinced you to do a rash deed and marry me."

She patted his chest, thinking what a good friend he was. "I'm in love with Miles, but if I wasn't, I would be very happy to marry you." She patted him again. "Are you carrying a flask inside your coat?"

"An armored plate over my heart," Frederick said. "Would you like a swig to fortify you before taking to the altar and making imprudent promises? I find that a pleasant haze makes agreeing to irrational demands more palatable."

"I take it fidelity is irrational?" Daisy asked.

"Fidelity would be easy," Frederick said, rather surprisingly for someone infamous for sleeping with married women. "It's the 'til death do us part' business that I find alarming. My valets always run off to greener pastures sooner or later, so I'd be unsurprised if my wife did the same."

"Where is Lord Devin?" Daisy's mother hissed, sweeping past them to welcome Lady Castlereigh with outstretched hands. "An informal occasion, my lady, since the children are so desperately in love!"

Frederick glanced around. "Devin lives next door, doesn't he? He can't blame a broken wheel or the traffic around Charing Cross."

Regina was greeting Viscount Peregrine and his wife, who had just entered the chapel.

"Peregrine was one of Regina's fiancés," Frederick said idly. "My brother was another, and your fiancé is a third. I've forgotten someone... Ah yes, the Earl of Winchester."

Daisy was starting to feel sick with anxiety. Surely Miles wouldn't stand her up at the altar. But perhaps he had found out the truth... Her mother's gloom-filled predictions crowded into her mind.

"Miles was never betrothed to Regina," she said, trying to focus on the conversation.

"I'll fetch your groom," Frederick said with sudden energy. "Best man's duty. Drag the poor sod to the altar." He blinked. "Not that he's a poor sod for marrying you. Luckiest man in London."

Before Daisy could say anything, he disappeared.

Five minutes later, two men walked into the chapel. "Found him redoing his cravat," Frederick boomed. "*Stop doting on your mirror, I told him. Your lovely bride is waiting.*"

Daisy knew Miles well enough to read the tightness at the corners of his stormy eyes, the nerve beating in his jaw. As their eyes met, his face was suddenly wreathed in one of the falsest smiles she'd ever seen.

"Darling," he said, heading straight toward her. "Forgive me."

Her heart stopped pounding. Miles's acting skills were dubious, but at least he had appeared. She put a hand on his cheek and smiled at him, letting all the adoration she felt shine in her eyes. He dropped his head and gave her a swift, hard kiss.

"Totally enamored," Regina said in a clear, high voice on the other side of the chapel.

As she spoke her vows, Daisy allowed herself only one aching wish that her groom loved her and that he'd been eager to marry her—rather than having trudged to the altar tardy and annoyed. Taking the long view, it was far more important that Miles would be loyal. She trusted him *to have and to hold, for better or worse,* even if he never managed the loving and cherishing.

After the ceremony, Lady Wharton ushered the guests away to enjoy the wedding breakfast, while Daisy, Miles, Regina and Frederick signed the parish book.

"Remain here two minutes, so you can make an entrance," Regina ordered, taking Frederick's arm and pulling him from the chapel.

"What happened?" Daisy asked bluntly. "Why were you late?"

Miles glanced at the rector, who was following Regina out the door. "Unforeseen circumstances."

Daisy swallowed hard and then came out with the truth. "I was afraid you weren't coming at all. People were beginning to chatter. If nothing else, your delay complicated Regina's description of you as besotted."

"I apologize." His jaw set again. "I shall do my best at breakfast to seem as happy as a pig in muck. I'll kiss you again in front of an audience, if you think that will stop them from chattering."

There couldn't be a more devastating contrast between the major's jubilant kiss and Miles's grudging offer.

"Is it so terrible to have people believe you're in love with me?" Daisy asked, her voice rasping.

"In my opinion, no one *will* believe it," Miles said coolly. "They'll think that your mother trapped me in some way or another. Most of them are intelligent enough to know that love is a temporary delusion."

Daisy took a deep breath. His words stung, but she couldn't poison their wedding day with a quarrel.

Besides, he was likely right about the aristocracy's assessment of their marriage. Lord Devin was rich, handsome, and powerful. In the eyes of society, he belonged with a diamond like Lady Regina, a woman with a superb profile fit for a family portrait.

Definitely *not* a plump, disheveled woman like Daisy. As if the universe heard that comment, a thick coil of hair slipped from her chignon and tumbled past her shoulder.

Miles's eyes suddenly focused on her face. "I apologize, Daisy. I had forgotten that you consider yourself in love with me. The emotion won't last. You do realize that, don't you?"

"More every moment," Daisy said wryly.

Unfortunately, freedom from that emotion lay in the future. At present, she merely had to glance at her husband, and her whole body pulsed with the urge to have and to hold him, through better or worse.

"It's not that you're not lovable," he added, making everything worse. "In fact, there are parts of you, Daisy, that are very lovable."

Parts of her? "Miles." The word scraped from her throat as she desperately tried to think how to tell him that her father always made her feel unlovable, and that she felt wretchedly inferior, marrying a man who only proposed under duress.

"Yes?"

"Please don't say things like that."

He frowned.

Daisy picked her words with care. "Our marriage follows a mistake I made. A terrible mistake. I took away your choice of a wife, and I'll always have to live with that. But *please* don't tell me again that you ... that you would never have chosen me."

"I didn't say that."

Daisy said doggedly, "When you say things such as, 'It could have been worse,' or say that only parts of me are lovable, it *hurts*. I couldn't bear it if my husband despised me."

"I would never despise you," Miles said, clearly irritated. "We should join our guests. Did you dress like the pillar of salt in a reference to Mrs. Lot's rebellion?"

She swallowed hard. Apparently the subject was closed. She felt a jolt of pure terror. This marriage threatened to break her, break her heart and her spirit. She tried to summon up a witticism. "Would you sulk if I had cast you in the role of Lot?"

"I'm more likely to run back to the city limits." One of his hands settled on the small of her back as he steered her through the chapel.

"No more depravity for you," she reminded him. If he left her and came back smelling of another woman's perfume? That *would* break her. She could not become her mother.

He stopped and looked down at her. Daisy felt a little wobble in her knees at his expression. "No public depravity," he confirmed. "But in our bedchamber?"

Just the sight of his lips was like running silk over her body. *All* of her body. When his lips landed on hers, she gasped. His tongue met hers, licked her delicately, withdrew.

Her heart stuttered. "That wasn't a real kiss."

Miles let out a crack of laughter. "Are real kisses required by new wives?" he asked.

Daisy didn't hesitate. "Absolutely."

A proper kiss, a drugging, deliriously sensual kiss, followed. Daisy's body turned molten with desire. Her fingers curled against the column of his neck, feeling the muscled power there.

How could a mere neck be so seductive? Her mind blurred as Miles drew back and nipped her bottom lip with his teeth. Instead of pushing him away, as any gently bred young lady would do, she pulled him closer.

Satin panels crushed as he moved to stand so close to her that their bodies touched.

"Oh," Daisy squeaked.

"Mmmm," her husband said. One of his hands curled around her bottom. "Your arse is a thing of beauty, Daisy. Did you know that? I wanted to marry you the moment this gown fell off. In fact, there's a satisfying symmetry in your wearing it this morning."

He began kissing her again, his tongue flicking around her mouth. Daisy's hands slid down to his sleeves, hanging on, her entire being focused on his kiss.

"I look forward to consummating our marriage, but we must wait until evening," Miles said. His eyes were hot as he rocked his hips forward again.

"Wait until—" Daisy lost track of the thought because that hand on her bottom was caressing her improperly, and it felt *so good.*

"Tonight," Miles said firmly, stepping backward.

Daisy looked at him, dazed.

"Perhaps I shall tear that gown off you, if only for nostalgia's sake."

Her eyes followed the movement of his hands at the front of his breeches. He rearranged himself with brutal casualness.

"I don't even have to worry about you enjoying yourself," he said with a distinct edge of anticipation. "I can tell that you know how to take your own pleasure."

"No," Daisy said breathlessly.

"No, you don't know how to take your pleasure?"

"Are you asking whether I have had an orgasm?" she asked.

"I take it that that sensation is not new to you," Miles said dryly.

Dairy felt her face turn even redder. "We mustn't have such an inappropriate conversation in a chapel." She began to shake out the satin panels of her gown, but they were hopelessly crumpled, hanging around her hips like the curled petals of a dying flower.

Embarrassingly, Miles was as elegant as when he'd first sauntered into the room with that ridiculous excuse about changing his cravat.

Other than the tent in the front of his breeches. *That* wasn't quite so elegant.

He bent to sweep up a few hairpins, handing them to her. "Frederick showed up at my place and offered to stand in as groom, by the way."

"When you didn't arrive on time, he proposed to me," Daisy began poking the pins into her chignon at random, hoping most of her hair would stay aloft. "You couldn't think of a better excuse than a cravat, Miles?"

"Be grateful that Frederick didn't mention a tow-headed baby."

Daisy gasped and dropped the pins she held. "He saw Belle?"

"He marched straight past Hobbs and walked into my bedchamber—where I was changing my cravat after Belle spit up milk. For her part, she was sitting on the floor, clinging to my leg and bellowing. During the night she decided that I was worth fighting for."

"Oh, no," Daisy breathed. "What did Frederick say when he saw Belle?"

"He raised an eyebrow and said, 'Wedding bells are ringing, or so they would be if you showed up.' Then he added something uncomplimentary that included a promise to cut my throat if I failed to shake off my child and make my vows in the next ten minutes, followed by an offer to replace me if I wished to run for the harbor."

A giggle escaped from Daisy's mouth, and she slapped a hand over her lips. "I'm sorry! It's not funny."

"I would have fired Hobbs for letting him upstairs, but I need the man to hire a nanny this afternoon. None of our maids was able to comfort the child, nor was the housekeeper. We need a miracle."

"I don't understand it. Belle seemed like such a happy baby."

"Perhaps she is, when she isn't teething. We'll have to tell the household carriage to drop back by a mile or we'll hear her howling."

Daisy grimaced. "I see shadows under your eyes. Did she wake you from sleep?"

A crack of laughter. "Sleep?"

Regina poked her head into the antechamber. "When I said to make an entrance, I didn't mean that you should wait an *hour*. Do come along. Everyone is titillated by a man with your fortune marrying in such haste," she told Miles. "Lady Wharton is telling people in strict confidence that she refused your first proposal but couldn't resist your second, after you fell to your knees and begged for Daisy's hand."

Miles looked disgusted.

"I thought you might need advance warning," Regina said smugly. "Keep in mind that you've been experiencing the agony of a broken heart for months."

"Could we announce that I stole my bride away after achieving my heart's desire?" Miles inquired.

Daisy felt the scorn in his voice like a blow.

"Not if you wish to quell the scandal," Regina said. "My brother lost his mind when he fell in love, so you can just copy his underbred mannerisms. Stare at your wife as if she hung the moon."

Miles looked as if he'd like to roll his eyes.

Why didn't she flee to Frederick's house, a man who was genuinely fond of her? Miles didn't seem to feel even a lukewarm version of that emotion.

Lust, yes. Affection? Perhaps.

"Come along, Lady Devin," her husband said resignedly, tucking her arm into his elbow. "I can't play this scene without a leading lady."

"Thank you again," she said, wondering if she would ever feel less guilty.

"Don't thank him! He seduced you, so it's the least he can do!" Regina said tartly, sweeping ahead of them to the door.

Episode 107: A Romeo for the Modern Day

The wedding breakfast was a triumph. Champagne flowed like water, while Lady Wharton flitted about the room spreading tales about Miles's supposedly intense emotions. He managed to bite back the sarcastic remarks that popped into his head every time a lady patted his arm, calling him a Romeo for the modern day.

Hopefully, by the time he returned to London, people would have forgotten that he was supposedly riddled with love to the point of threatening to injure himself—like a damn fool.

Daisy's infatuation did give the event an air of veracity. Every single time he put a hand on her back, rosy color crept into her cheeks. He found it fairly easy to play the role of a lovesick husband—Daisy was so pretty and charming that he kept having to intervene with men trying to flirt with his new bride—but anyone could tell that *her* emotion was genuine. Not something he ever envisioned in a wife, but it was rather pleasant nonetheless.

Finally Lady Wharton nodded, the signal that he and his wife were allowed to depart. He caught Daisy's hand and then froze, struck by the glow in her eyes as she smiled at him.

His wife was in love with him.

Amazing.

"Time to leave," he said.

Daisy curtsied before Viscount Peregrine. "If you'll excuse me, my lord."

Peregrine was a somber fellow, one who—thankfully—had never come before Miles in a criminal capacity. In fact, Miles had the distinct idea that the viscount was ethical to the bone, not a quality he saw often.

"Say no more," Peregrine said, a faint smile in his eyes. "My wife and I are still newlyweds ourselves." The viscountess was extremely pretty, especially as she smiled up at her husband.

Miles had *that* now. A woman who smiled at him like that.

Suddenly inspired, he swept Daisy up in his arms. Her gown didn't rip, though panels of white satin fell over his arms.

"Miles!" she hissed. "What on earth are you doing?"

"Playing the part of Romeo." He looked around the people in the room, collecting gazes. "Lady Devin and I are leaving, with gratitude for your attendance at our wedding. I apologize for the short notice." He dropped a kiss on her nose. "Daisy turned me down a few months ago, and when she finally said yes, I was terrified that she would change her mind."

Daisy began giggling, one arm around his neck. "Goodbye!" she called.

Miles walked out of the room to the sound of applause.

Once they left Regina's house, Daisy said, "You can put me down now, Miles."

"They might be watching from the windows," he said, tramping over the lawn that separated his house from the Duke of Lennox's.

Daisy was caught by the strange feeling that she was not living her life but watching it. From the duke's windows, a groom carrying his bride must seem wildly romantic. In reality? She felt like a hefty bundle of laundry being hauled to the washhouse.

"Your arms must be aching."

"Not at all." He cocked his ear. "I don't hear any screaming coming from the nursery, do you? Perhaps the tooth cut through."

"That sounds violent," Daisy said, realizing how much she had to learn about raising children.

Miles shrugged. "Once a tooth can be seen, there'll be no more wailing. I might as well tell you that when Belle was still screaming at dawn, I decided that we might as well head directly for my county seat after the ceremony."

"Of course, we should leave immediately," Daisy agreed.

He headed for the front steps. "I've changed my mind. Based on our behavior in the chapel, I have the distinct impression that you and I alone in a carriage would result in connubial relations while jolting up and down on the toll road."

Daisy felt herself turning pink. She cleared her throat but couldn't think what to say. She'd never imagined people making love in carriages.

Her husband gave her a wicked grin. "All the movement should be mine, don't you think?"

Why did she feel like arguing with him? She had absolutely no experience—no matter what Miles thought—but *City of Eros* talked about a woman bouncing on top of a man. Why should all the movement be his?

Miles cleared his throat. "I'm going to have to get used to this." His voice was ripe with devilish amusement.

"What?"

"You don't agree with me, do you? We're lucky."

"Because?"

"Bedding is the glue that holds couples together. That and honesty."

Daisy managed a tremulous smile. But inside? Her heart was beating painfully fast. Yes, they had lust, but not love. They didn't have honesty, either, since she had lied to him. Not to mention the fact that he was so thrilled about the erotic experience she didn't have.

"We should discuss Belle," she said, taking a deep breath. It was time to come clean.

"No, we shouldn't," Miles said decisively. "Where is Hobbs? Is it too much to ask that he keep an eye on the front door?" He gave it a kick, leaving a scuff on the white paint.

"I could have knocked, or you could have put me down," Daisy pointed out.

"I'm carrying you over the threshold," he said gruffly. Then he blinked. "I apologize. Lack of sleep makes me irritable. The truth is that

I don't want to talk about Belle's father. She is an orphan, soon to be my ward. I grew fond of her last night—irrationally, since she spent most of it howling. Her parentage is irrelevant because she's mine. And yours, obviously."

Hobbs opened the door, stepped back, and bowed.

"Finally," Miles said, carrying Daisy into a spacious marble entry. "Your new mistress, Hobbs. Lady Devin." He set Daisy down with a thump.

Her sympathy with sacks of laundry was increasing by the moment.

"My lady," Hobbs said, bowing. "I bid you welcome to Devin House." Behind him, two maids came running down the stairs, and several footmen emerged from the baize door that led downstairs, clustering behind Hobbs.

"Have you been in Lord Devin's employ for a long time?" Daisy asked, thinking of Miles's threat to fire him. The butler looked too elderly to find another post.

"Years," Hobbs said with pride. "His lordship keeps trying to pension me off, but I knew him as a nipper, and I shan't resign until I want to."

"You're a pain in my arse," Miles said.

"His lordship doesn't take well to lack of sleep," Hobbs said with a confidential twitch of his eyebrow. "The young lass, Miss Belle, had a tooth paining her, and Lord Devin walked the floor like the old days. Miss Clementine never liked to cut a tooth."

Miles growled something under his breath, but Hobbs ignored him. "May I introduce the household, my lady? This is Mrs. Bretton, our housekeeper..."

When Hobbs introduced her to the maid Daisy had last seen holding the baby, the poor girl looked exhausted.

"I'm so sorry that Belle kept you awake," Daisy said.

The maid curtsied. "She's taken a dislike to me, my lady. No one but Lord Devin could persuade her to stop crying. Thankfully, that tooth finally came through an hour ago."

"Thank God," Miles said.

"Miss Belle has had some warm milk and is fast sleep," Mrs. Bretton put in.

No one in the household was wary of Miles, and unless she was mistaken, they truly liked him. "Marvelous," Daisy said warmly. "I hope that my personal maid, Ada, has been introduced to everyone?"

"An Irish lass is always welcome here," Hobbs proclaimed. "She is in your bedchamber, arranging your bits and bobs, my lady."

"I shall escort you upstairs," Miles declared. Once they climbed the stairs, he pushed open a door to reveal a large bedchamber at the rear of the house with recessed windows facing a lawn studded by gracious oak trees.

Most of the room was taken up by an extremely large bed, so high that a short flight of stairs awaited its occupants.

Daisy quickly looked away from the mounds of snowy pillows. "A place to read!" she exclaimed, darting across the room to the comfortable window seat surrounded by bookshelves.

Ada popped out of a side door, but Miles left before Daisy could introduce her. In fact, Daisy wheeled about just in time to see the door shut behind him.

"The marriage won't be consummated until evening," she blurted out, with a distinct sense of relief. It wasn't the bedding that worried her; it was all the confessions she had to make first.

Ada let out a giggle. "It's kind of his lordship to give you time to prepare."

"Perhaps," Daisy said. She was so rattled that her next thought spilled out. "A besotted man wouldn't run away. I expect Livie's husband carried *her* over the threshold to their bedchamber and didn't leave until morning."

"Yes, but Lord Devin is a perfect gentleman. Always considerate, that's what they say below stairs."

Daisy didn't think she'd experienced Miles's considerate side. Being informed that only parts of her were lovable had definitely cast a shadow over the morning.

"Did you warn them that I am not a perfect lady?"

"You'll be a breath of fresh air," Ada said tactfully. "I've run a bath in the water closet. Mr. Hobbs sent your trunks straight to the country, but I've kept back a traveling gown and that blue gown you like for tonight."

Unlike so many dresses ordered under the aegis of her mother, this one was cut to a fashionable length.

Daisy nodded and wandered into the water closet, a spacious room with a dressing table, its own fireplace, and a ceramic bathtub that filled with water heated by the kitchen chimney. Ten minutes later she was up to her chin in a warm bath.

"I love the fragrance of this soap," she said, trying to relax. Nothing would happen before evening. She could bathe, go downstairs, and calmly inform Miles that she had fibbed about a few things. Unimportant things. Relatively unimportant things.

"Wild cherry," Ada replied, carefully arranging Daisy's toiletries. "I heard all about it this morning. Lord Devin's mother had a great love for country matters. She enjoyed experimenting with soaps and lotions and tending honeybees. Are you likely to follow in her footsteps, my lady?"

"No. I haven't the faintest idea how to make soap, and I dislike being stung by bees." She stretched one leg out of the water, wishing that she had Regina's slender limbs rather than thick thighs. "You know what I'm like, Ada. I like to read novels. I'm frivolous by nature and inclination, and I do not intend to allow marriage to change me."

"That's all right," Ada said. "The late Lady Devin passed away years ago, and the housekeeper has used the lady's recipe to make soap ever since. Mrs. Bretton seems rigid but fair. I expect she'll welcome a mistress who doesn't care to alter her routine."

"I shan't interfere." Daisy had never given much thought to her mother's propensity to live in London rather than the country estate, though now she understood that Lady Wharton had been avoiding her husband. The upshot was that Daisy had no idea how landed gentry behaved outside the city, though surely they didn't make soap all day.

"Did they tell you anything else about the late Lady Devin?"

"She had a swanlike beauty," Ada said promptly "That's the word Mr. Hobbs used, 'swanlike.'"

Daisy sighed. "I could achieve a chicken—one with a crest of feathers—but never a swan."

"Mr. Hobbs remarked on your beautiful hair."

Daisy peered at her from under a huge crown of soap bubbles. "It's a nuisance. Look how many hairpins I've lost over the years. Several tinkled on the chapel floor as I was walking the aisle."

Ada laughed. "I told the housekeeper that we need to buy them in bulk."

A few minutes later, Daisy sat down before the fire, wringing water from the rope of hair that hung over her shoulder. Ada began combing in scented oil to keep her curls from frizzing as they dried.

"Daisy?"

Miles's voice came from the bedchamber. Her heart skipped a beat.

"My lady," Ada hissed. "It's him!"

Daisy got to her feet, winding the toweling more tightly around her breasts. She had a feeling of raw panic. Time to face the music.

Own up to mistakes.

Consummate the marriage?

Episode 108: Consummation?

Miles strolled into his wife's bedroom, aware that every part of his body was standing at attention. He had planned to consummate his marriage in the evening. Only an infatuated fool couldn't curb his lust for a few hours.

He had waited one hour. A gentlemanly hour. He'd had a bath, shaved, put on clean garments, and decided that gentleman or not, he couldn't wait. The chamber was empty, but he heard the murmur of women's voices from the water closet. "Daisy?"

His wife walked into the bedroom a moment later, and the nerves that had been sparking in his body raged into a forest fire. He felt as eager as a young man seeing a naked woman for the first time, his heart beating so hard that he fancied his shirt front was vibrating. He only vaguely noticed as her maid dipped a curtsy and trotted out the door.

Daisy's curves were emphasized by toweling wound tightly around her body. Her lips were plump and luscious, her chin pointed, her nose snub, her cheeks—

"You are incredibly beautiful." The words leapt from his mouth without conscious volition.

Color flared higher in her cheeks. "Miles. You're ... here. In my bedchamber."

He couldn't bring himself to obfuscate. "Yes. I thought perhaps we could go to bed."

Daisy glanced at the sunshine pouring into the room. "You said we would wait until nightfall." She turned even pinker. "Everyone will know what we're doing."

"Most newlyweds rush toward the nearest bed." His voice had an embarrassingly hungry rumble. He took a few steps toward her. "But we could wait if you'd prefer." Conscience prickled him. "For that matter, we needn't consummate the marriage until you feel comfortable, Daisy. It's up to you."

His new wife couldn't turn any redder. Daisy looked…not afraid, but cautious. Not nervous, but not experienced, either.

It occurred to him that she looked like a virgin, but that was absurd. What did he know of virgins, anyway? His erotic history had played out with dancers who dressed as flowers precisely because it was easy to drop their petals.

Daisy cleared her throat. "All right. But first I'd like to talk."

Her response wasn't precisely enthusiastic, but Miles had no intention of arguing. He promptly began unbuttoning his coat. "I'm happy to talk." Hopefully she didn't want to tell him about her former lover. He'd pulled off his shirt before he noticed how tightly Daisy was clutching her towel.

He strolled closer and ran a finger over her white knuckles. "Would you like something to drink? We could ring for champagne."

"I'd rather have a clear head. Could we have a cup of tea?"

He burst out laughing.

"I suppose that request might startle the household," Daisy conceded.

"It does lend itself to the suggestion that you are bracing yourself."

She backed away. "I suspect any number of women long for a cup of tea as the wedding night approaches. Just imagine if we had to have a bedding ceremony."

Miles raised an eyebrow. "During which the whole village tucks a man and wife under the sheets? I'd need something stronger than tea."

Some of the color had faded from her cheeks. She nodded toward his chest. "Very impressive musculature for a gentleman."

Just how many men was he being compared to? Miles choked back that unfair, jealous thought. Daisy had come to him with her baby. She trusted him. "Thank you."

"Was it improper of me to comment? I don't know how to behave like a wife, for obvious reasons."

"I don't know how to be a husband," Miles said, realizing it was true. "My parents died long ago."

"Don't model yourself on my father, and you'll already be ahead," Daisy said wryly. "Or Livie's," she added.

"I have not committed homicide, and as yet I've had little inclination to do so," Miles said, though in the back of his mind, he reserved the right to slay her married lover, if he ever found out the lout's name.

He moved to stand just before her and bent to whisper his lips over hers. The tip of her tongue slid along his lower lip. Belying the light touch, it felt like a burn scalded his body, racing down his spine, wrapping around his loins. Hungry yearning took hold of him, wiping everything from his mind but his wife's curves.

His hands wrapped around her waist, and he lifted her to the edge of the bed so that he could kiss her easily.

"You mustn't get the habit of carrying me around," Daisy observed. "I'm not a bag of laundry."

"I won't," he muttered, gently tipping her backwards. As he braced his arms on the mattress on either side of her, her full, soft breasts flattened against his chest. His lips hovered over hers.

They were silent, looking into each other's eyes for long enough to become awkward, but Miles couldn't find any words. His mind—his body—was focused on Daisy rather than on shaping language.

"Kiss me," she said finally, her voice raspy and deep. "Then we'll talk."

Miles didn't follow orders very often; he rarely received them. But his lips covered hers so quickly that he caught the sound of "talk" with his tongue.

Kissing his wife was like kissing a firecracker. The impulsivity and brightness, the sparkle that made Daisy into... *Daisy,* shot through his body as their tongue knit together. The kiss wasn't sensitive and sweet, but wild and demanding. One of his hands slid over the toweling, reached her plump arse, and curved around it, pulling her even closer. Their tongues stroked until she broke free with a strangled gasp for air.

Miles let her breathe, lowering his head to kiss her jawline before his hands cupped her face and tilted her head back so that he could ravage her mouth again, his broad tool pressing into her warmth.

A soft alarm sounded in his head, warning that her taste was like a drug. Ignoring it, Miles trailed his mouth over her closed eyelids, sliding his hands around the elegant frame of her head, arrowing his fingers into her hair. It was still damp, curling around his fingers.

Daisy's eyes opened, lashes fluttering. She didn't look alarmed or frightened, but as desirous as he. "May I?" he asked, hooking a finger into the toweling that miraculously had remained wrapped around her body.

She blinked and shook her head. "Not yet. I want to talk before we ... "

He nodded. "In a few minutes." Her hands were soothing his chest, fingers spread wide like starfish. They brushed his nipples, and his whole body jolted.

Fever bright eyes met his. "Do you like that?" Daisy whispered. Her hands swept down the sides of his body to the top of his breeches. "You have remarkable muscles."

The words jumped out of his mouth. "Compared to?"

"When I was fourteen, I saw a groom washing himself in the horse trough." She shot him a naughty look that made his cock pulse against his silk breeches. "I watched for longer than I ought to have, so I have clear memories of his chest. But you ... "

"I wasn't always this burly," he admitted. "In the last year, I've worked off the stresses of my position at the House of Lords by frequenting Gentleman Jack's Boxing Salon almost every day."

"I would say *rugged* rather than *burly*."

Miles tugged gently at her toweling, eyebrow raised. "Please?"

She swallowed visibly, then gave a tiny nod, her fingers curling around the waistband of his breeches, touching skin that prickled into life.

Carefully Miles untucked her towel and drew the two sides apart. Daisy was ... luscious. Utterly luscious, with generous curves and skin like cream roses, dotted here and there by little brown dots that he wanted to lick. Her nipples were raspberries, and the curls between her legs only slightly darker than the hair on her head.

On her hips were silver streaks, evidence of the child she carried. He ran his fingers over them, thinking that someday Daisy would carry his child. "I will love Belle," he said abruptly.

Daisy frowned, looking down at his hands. "What?"

"These marks are from carrying Belle, are they not?" He smoothed his fingers over them again. A wash of gratitude went through him. So many women were lost in childbirth. His wife was fertile and had carried a baby to term.

"No," Daisy said bluntly. "Those have nothing to do with a child. They appeared when I was a girl, as my hips grew."

His hands curled around her hips, fingers sinking into warm flesh, easing her closer to the edge of the bed so he could kneel and worship her with his mouth. His body shuddered with anticipation, thinking of that intimate caress.

"I love your hips," he rumbled. Some dim part of his brain reminded him that Daisy had asked for tea and conversation, not a husband who leaped on her like a lion on a gazelle. He cleared his throat. "Was there something you'd like to discuss before we continue?"

She came up on her elbows, looking at him. "Do you wish that I was a virgin?" Her eyes sparkled at him with an odd sense of suppressed excitement. "Every man wishes that in his wife, doesn't he?"

Obviously, the topic was delicate. Miles hesitated. Social norms governing women's erotic lives were unfair, yet some uncivilized part of him had loved the idea that his wife would be his alone.

He decided to dodge the question. "Marrying a virgin would be a risk. What if she saw my burly chest and shuddered with disgust? What if she insisted on making love under cover of darkness? What if she took no pleasure in our bed?"

"Couldn't you have taught her pleasure?"

"I could try, but believe me, it's a rare gentleman who is lucky in that regard."

His wife was biting her bottom lip so hard that it had turned cherry red. Obviously, Daisy felt shamed by her lack of chastity. "What if I terrified my bride?"

Her brows drew together. "What do you mean?"

Miles undid his placket and drew out his tool. It bobbed against his stomach. Her eyes widened, and she drew in a silent breath.

"We *will* fit, but a virgin might well faint at the sight. That's added to the fact that she wouldn't know how to find her own pleasure."

She rolled her eyes. "A male appendage is not necessary for pleasure."

Miles grinned at her. "You see? I am so damn lucky because you like my burly chest and hopefully the rest of me, and you've already given birth to a child, so I needn't worry about you dying in childbirth—"

"Miles," she interrupted.

"Yes?"

"I have to tell you something."

Episode 109:
The Lies. Two of Them.

*D*aisy was caught between embarrassment and desire. She had been certain that Miles would be happy to learn that she was chaste, but her mother's prophecies were making her nervous.

She sat upright as his palms curled around her knees, nudging them gently apart.

"Yes?"

"I'm a virgin."

Miles's eyes had been fixed on her thighs—or perhaps between her thighs—but now he looked up, brows drawing together. "What did you say?"

"Belle isn't mine. I'm a virgin," she repeated.

His hands fell away, and he stepped back, his face snapping into rigidity. "Belle is *not your child*?"

Her breath caught as she nodded. "I hope you're pleased."

Silence. Then:

"You hope I'm *pleased* that I married my wife under false pretenses?" It wasn't precisely a bellow, but close.

"That's not exactly—"

"That is exactly how it is," Miles said harshly. "Why in the hell did you bring the child to my house?" His eyes narrowed. "Your half-sister, presumably?"

"I didn't think," Daisy said, a familiar wash of embarrassment sending a red flush up her breasts. She glanced down and snatched the sides of the towel, covering up her body. "My mother planned to send Belle to an orphanage."

His frown deepened. "You must be joking."

"Belle was not the first child delivered to our doorstep," Daisy said, humiliation making her bones feel heavy as stone. "My father has no interest in their care, so my mother dispatches his children to an orphanage."

"Marvelous," Miles said, clearly in a profound rage. "What an ethical, caring family I've married into."

Daisy let that go. He had the right.

"I had no idea that my half-siblings existed until I discovered Belle on our doorstep. Our butler was coming to take her away, so I ran out of the house and brought her to you."

After a grim silence, he said, "To call a stone a stone, since you had an infatuation with me, I was the lucky man graced with you *and* the baby, whom you then used to force me to marry you by pretending that you had been seduced."

Daisy began trembling from another blast of shame. His eyes felt as if they seared through her, looking at her very soul and finding it wanting. "No!" she cried. "That wasn't it at all! Our marriage only happened because Regina entered the room."

But inside she quailed. Hadn't she in fact chosen to go to Miles over Frederick precisely because she *was* in love with him?

Obviously he saw guilt in her face. His lip curled as he turned away.

"You are so good at solving problems," Daisy whispered, looking down at her fingers twisting together. "I panicked." Regret felt like a mantle of black soot closing around her.

"This reminds me of when you smuggled a file into the Tower of London. If you had given any thought to your actions, you would have guessed that your uncle would be severely punished if found in possession of such an implement. But no, you rashly went ahead because you had a stupid idea and didn't think it through!"

Miles wasn't wrong. She'd thought a file was a funny gift for a prisoner, never for a moment believing that her pompous uncle would wiggle through a narrow window—or that he might be punished for its possession. Luckily Miles confiscated it before it reached her uncle's hands.

"I knew nothing of prisons. I just thought it might raise his spirits." Her voice cracked. "I don't think it's fair to compare my uncle's possible fate—had you not confiscated the file—to you marrying me."

"A life sentence in both cases," Miles said, with crushing effect. He spun about and bent to snatch up his breeches.

Daisy stared at his muscled arse. She was such a fool. Even now, when he was livid at her, desire sizzled in her core. "I didn't mean to imprison you in a marital tower, if that's what you're implying."

"Really? There's no escaping marriage," Miles growled. "We have to live with the outcome of your impulsive decision, so do your motivations matter? You said, 'The baby is mine!' Why didn't you simply tell the truth? It would have been easy enough to admit that Belle is your father's bastard offspring. Frankly, it wouldn't been shocked me, given his reputation. Lady Regina may have been stunned initially, but surprised? Unlikely."

"I was trying to protect *you* by saying the baby was mine, since Regina was assuming that Belle was yours, and it all went wrong." She let out a sobbing breath. "Please believe me, Miles."

How could she have fallen in love with a man who could look at her so coldly that it made her stomach clench? Her mind spun between a shameful conviction that she deserved his condemnation to a rebellious feeling that events beyond their control had swept both of them off their feet.

"I did not arrive at your house with a Machiavellian plan spurred by my . . . my short-lived infatuation," she added, registering that her skin had gone from heated to clammy and cold.

He yanked his shirt over his head. "Short-lived, eh? Another impulsive decision that you've rethought, Daisy?"

"You said this morning that you didn't despise me." She forced the words from her throat.

Miles didn't even look at her. "To clarify: I despise your behavior."

Perhaps she should slide off the bed and face him, as if they were gladiators in a Roman amphitheater. But she was so much shorter than he was.

"You could—you might think of my visit as a compliment,'" she said, summoning up a defense. "I turned to you when I faced a crisis. Your parents left care of your sisters to you, though you were still a boy, knowing that you would be an excellent brother and stand-in parent."

"Why didn't you turn to the obvious person, your father?" Miles demanded. "If you were afraid to do so, you could have relegated that unpleasant duty to me. If you'd told me the truth, I would have found the worthless philistine and made him take charge of his responsibilities for once in his life—just as I'm about to do."

Daisy opened her mouth, and he snapped, "Be quiet. Don't make things worse. *Think before you say anything!*"

"Belle would have been taken away from me," she whispered.

A groundswell of anger began to bubble inside her. She watched silently as he wrenched on the rest of his clothing, stamping into his boots. He was an ass. She had claimed Belle was hers partly in an effort to protect him, which backfired. Did that make her stupid?

"Are you truly going to see my father?"

"Yes," he snarled. "Wharton is going to stand up and be counted. I inherited my little sisters when I was *fourteen*, and I managed. So can he."

"You're ... you're giving Belle to him?"

"Hell, yes. That wretched blackguard is going to care for his latest bastard. What's more, he can support every child of his dropped at an orphanage. I am revolted by his monstrous, lackadaisical attitude toward his responsibilities."

"I understand your point of view," Daisy said, looking at Miles through new eyes. How could he be quick to ship Belle off to her indolent father after soothing her all night long? Was he really so bloodless and uncaring? "But she is my child," she said doggedly, holding onto that thought.

"The hell she is! She isn't a child of your body. She's a prostitute's get, and your father's, if she's anyone's. She is *not yours*." Miles tied his cravat with abrupt, furious turns, not even looking in a glass.

"I didn't think you had such brutality in you," she said. "I thought you had come to care for Belle."

The words fell into the space between them and stayed there, hanging in the air.

"I live up to my obligations," Miles said with chilling emphasis. "I spend my days investigating men—*gentlemen*—who use their birth and their position to avoid adhering to the most basic rules of civilization, one of which is that a man must care for his children."

His voice echoed in Daisy's head like cannon fire in a ravine. He wasn't wrong. Her father should retrieve and support the children relegated to orphanages.

But Lord Wharton couldn't have Belle.

Miles turned to the mirror above the fireplace, his elegant coat belling out behind him as he pulled down his cuffs.

Daisy watched mutely. She had said what needed to be said. He could storm off and deal with her father—while she and Belle would leave.

She needed rusks, nappies, and money—a great deal of money. Luckily, over the years she rarely used her allowance, instead tucking hundreds of pounds in the bottom of her jewelry box. It should be enough to take her to Brussels, where Livie and her husband were living.

"You are dangerously silent," Miles commented, a sardonic edge to his voice. "No further justification?"

He was an *arse*. The worst man of her acquaintance.

"You're the only man I've heard of who would be unhappy to discover that his bride is an innocent." Not that she intended to be his wife for long.

"You don't understand. You're a *liar*, Daisy. You lie easily to get your way. You lie about the most important things—about Belle's parentage. Who wants that in a wife?"

Daisy flinched. "I couldn't tell you who her father was because you threatened to kill the man. He's my father as well."

"He's scum," Miles said contemptuously.

Lord Wharton might be scum, but he was her scum. Besides, it didn't matter. Her husband thought she was scum as well, so why bother defending her actions? All the same, she couldn't stop herself from trying to explain again.

"When Regina entered and saw you with the baby, I wasn't manipulating the situation, as you seem to think. I just... I just spoke from the heart. Belle *is* my baby."

"You spoke impulsively? What a surprise." He narrowed his eyes.

"I think you've made your point as regards my lack of forethought," Daisy said, her jaw set. She wasn't infatuated anymore; in fact, she hated him.

"How angry are you?"

"Very," she stated.

He sighed.

"Oh, did you want me to lie to you?" she asked sweetly. "I'm sorry, I'm clean out of falsehoods at the moment."

"We can talk tonight," Miles repeated. He was at the door, but turned and walked back. "After we consummate our marriage."

Daisy looked at him in disbelief.

He shocked her by pulling her into an urgent, hungry kiss. Despite herself, Daisy opened her mouth, loving the taste and the smell of him.

It was probably their last kiss, so she tried to memorize every sensation: the slight prickle of his beard under her fingers, the hungry heat of his mouth, the way his big hands cupped the back of her head.

He smelled like safety and home.

Yet it would break her heart and her spirit to stay in a broken marriage, one in which the husband felt like a prisoner, trapped by his wife's falsehoods. In which he looked at her with such scorn and distaste.

The mortifying truth was that she deserved his distaste. She *had* lied. Her mother had been right. Her virginity wasn't enough to make up for what she did to Miles, and now his rage would be between them forever, especially after his interest in bedding her waned. She could already feel him fighting the desire that flared between them.

She pulled back, looking at his broad jaw, the blade of his nose, his distrustful eyes. Her heart felt as if a skewer had gone through it.

"This is exactly what I asked you not to do," she whispered.

"Kiss you? More the opposite, as I recall," he drawled. He straightened, pulling his hands through his hair.

"I asked you not to make me feel despised and unlovable."

"Surely you didn't think that I would happily accept the news that you had lied to me?"

She was such a fool.

He agreed with her assessment: she saw it in his eyes. She could not stay here, loving a man who despised her...

Perhaps especially because he had every right to.

Episode 110: Escape

Twenty minutes after Miles left her bedchamber, Daisy made her way down to the entry of Devin House. Belle was wrapped in her satin-trimmed blanket and tucked in the crook of her arm. Ada followed, carrying Belle's basket, which now held a jewelry box and a bag of rusks.

Hobbs was wringing his hands. "The master's had no sleep, my lady. He's got a tiger's snarl when he's exhausted, but he didn't mean whatever he said."

Daisy managed a smile. "Our marriage was a mistake, Hobbs. A rash, impulsive blunder, but one easily solved by an annulment. I'd be grateful if you'd have my clothing sent back from the country. Please tell Lord Devin that I left a letter for him on my dressing table."

"Shall we return to your mother?" Ada asked, as Mrs. Bretton handed her a satchel containing nappies and baby clothing.

"No." That was the first place Miles would look, if only to blast her for impulsively leaving him. "We'll stay with a friend."

"I don't believe a marriage is easily annulled," Ada commented, once they had climbed into a hackney carriage. "Though perhaps the process is simpler when a husband storms out before consummation," she added thoughtfully. "I haven't heard of that happening before."

"I'm certain that's the case. It's not yet legal." Belle stuck her thumb in her mouth and gave a huge sigh, so Daisy started crooning a lullaby.

"If I hadn't been told otherwise, I would swear Belle was your baby," Ada commented. "She looks like a miniature version of you."

Daisy glanced down at the baby's white-blonde curls. "She *is* mine. I plan to move to Brussels where my cousin lives. I would be very grateful if you would travel with me, Ada. It's not a long sea voyage, and I'll pay your passage there and back."

"You couldn't do it without me," Ada said practically. "Are you certain you want to leave Lord Devin? Everyone down to the boot boy says he's generous and fair. Not to mention rich. I'd marry him for the bathtub alone, and that's not taking into account his thighs." She laughed.

"He's very angry at me," Daisy said. "I don't blame him, but I can't live with him under those circumstances."

"So what set him off, then?" Ada looked at Daisy expectantly. "Being an Irishman, my father used to explode like one of them new firecrackers. In his case, it was always a matter of the belly. If he was hungry...look out!"

"I married Lord Devin under false pretenses. I told him Belle was my own child."

Ada frowned. "That's absurd. He came around to the house when you were working on those coded letters with Lord FitzRoy-Paget last year. You weren't showing. By the trial, you'd have been swollen like a gourd. What's more, Belle was likely born in February, and the ball where your dress fell apart was early March. Surely he doesn't think that ladies prance straight from the birthing chamber to the ballroom?"

Daisy shrugged. "Why would he know anything about pregnancy? I certainly don't."

"Everyone knows it takes nine months to grow a child," Ada objected.

"I was so stupid," Daisy confessed. "I actually thought that he'd be happy to discover I was a virgin. Instead he is furious and thinks I manipulated him into marriage."

"That *is* surprising," Ada said, nodding. "The way men go on about chastity and obedience from the pulpit, you'd think that a woman turned into a clod of dirt the moment she allowed a man between her legs."

Daisy rocked Belle gently back and forth.

"I could have sworn Lord Devin was mad about you," her maid added. "The way he looked at you this morning! I had to fan myself after I left the room."

"You'd be wrong," Daisy said flatly. "He didn't even stay around long enough to bed me, and that speaks for itself, doesn't it?"

Ada winced. "Aye, I'm afraid that it does.

"As soon as he heard the truth, he put his clothes back on and left me sitting on the bed." Daisy's voice cracked.

Ada's eyes rounded. "You were still in that towel?"

"Not even. And he was in the buff himself."

"Where did he go tearing off to, then?"

"He left to chastise Belle's father."

"Lord Devin put his clothes back on, the better to go out and have a fight with your Da?"

Daisy blinked.

"Everyone in Lady Wharton's household knows about the babes," Ada said, leaning forward to pat Daisy's knee. "Your father is infamous for his nighttime activities. Not to mention those other children that appeared over the years, all of them your spitting image."

"My mother is convinced that only our butler knows of the orphans," Daisy said, shocked to the bone.

"They aren't orphans, though, are they? There's been some debate below stairs about that. Still, even those who didn't think Lady Wharton should have sent the babes to an orphanage are loyal to her, sorry that she married a man like your father. He must walk into a brothel the way fox does a henhouse, if you'll forgive the vulgarity."

"I had no idea what he was truly like," Daisy said. Then she sighed. "I definitely married a man who is the opposite of my father."

Ada snorted. "Aye, that's right. There's scarcely a man in a hundred who would have left you, just out of the bath, naked as the day is long."

"Lucky me, I found that very man," Daisy said. A lump in her throat was making it hard to swallow.

"Don't look like that!" Ada said. "Don't go thinking it's anything to do with you."

"I'm not," Daisy said, untruthfully.

Lust was obviously fleeting: men felt it for any woman who flounced up to them in a brothel. What man would leave a naked woman on the bed—unless he was basically uninterested in bedding her?

Miles wouldn't have walked out on Regina, who had no resemblance to a sack of laundry.

Daisy would have loved to cry, but she couldn't. She was holding a sleeping baby, *her* baby, so the horrible ache in her chest had to be suppressed. That's what mothers did.

When she and Ada climbed out of the carriage, Frederick's butler, Mr. Oates-Plagitt, rushed out the door. "Miss Wharton! I mean, Lady Devin."

"Miss Wharton will do," Daisy said quietly, trying not to wake Belle. "Is Frederick at home, Oates-Plagitt?"

"He is."

"Sober?" She caught the butler's expression. "Oh, not entirely," she clarified. "But well enough to string three words together?"

"Definitely sober enough for that. He's in the library."

"Excellent. Can you please make sure that Ada and Belle are comfortable?" She hesitated. "I would be grateful if a maid could be assigned to care for my daughter."

My daughter. It was the first time she had said those words outside of hers or Miles's household.

"Certainly," Oates-Plagitt said. "The nursery is newly refurbished. I think the young miss will be very happy there."

She raised an eyebrow. "Was that due to Livie marrying Major FitzRoy?"

"No." Oates-Plagitt gave her a wry smile. "Master Frederick was hopeful that you'd accept his proposal."

"He never properly asked me." But the truth was that she could never marry Frederick, because she'd been stupid enough to fall in love with a disinterested man. Moving to Brussels, her not-so-precious virginity intact, would be better than staying anywhere in her husband's vicinity.

Ada deftly took the sleeping baby and followed Oates-Plagitt up the stairs to the nursery while Daisy went down the hallway to the library. She found Frederick comfortably stretched out on a sofa before the fire, his booted feet crossed over one arm and his head on the other, deep in a book. A glass of whiskey and a bowl of apples sat on the floor within easy reach of his hand.

Even miserable as she felt, the sight of her friend made her smile. "Among gentlefolk, likely you and I are the most habitually disheveled," she observed, walking over to him.

Frederick looked up at her, brow knitted, eyes slowly focusing. "What are you doing here, dear girl? Or should I say, Lady Devin?"

It hurt to laugh. "Not for long."

"What in the bloody hell happened?" Frederick asked. He sprang to his feet and swayed for a moment. "He figured out, didn't he? Here, sit down."

"Figured out what?" Daisy sank onto the couch.

"Drink this." Frederick pushed his glass into her hand.

"I don't like whiskey."

"It's apple juice. I haven't touched it, because I hate apples."

Daisy frowned, looking down at the bowl at their feet.

"Oates-Plagitt read in some infernal pamphlet that apples stop a man from thirsting for spirits. My personal experience is that they choke you with sweetness and do nothing for your appreciation of a fine Calvados."

He pulled her down to sit with him. "Back to the point, dear. Devin figured out, didn't he? I suppose he's enraged."

Daisy was so tired that she felt dizzy; the wedding that morning felt as if it had happened a year ago. She frowned at Frederick. "How did you know? What do you know?"

"Well, your husband thinks that child—Belle, isn't she? Devin thinks that Belle is yours, which just goes to show what idiots men are. To particularize that observation: his lordship is an idiot."

"How did *you* realize she is not mine?" Daisy asked. "My mother would never have betrayed that information."

"I established it on the grounds of mathematics, economics, and perception. Mathematically, you've had no time to carry a child for nine months, give birth to it, and gallop back to the ballroom to debut. Devin and I spent sufficient time with you last year to see an expanding waistline, had there been one to see. Turning to economics, your mother has plenty of money. She would never put a soiled dove on the marriage market; she would have bought you a husband."

"I see," Daisy said. "Perception?"

"You're innocent," Frederick said. "Any man who's paying close attention to you would know that. You have a spark of humor that can be mistaken for experience, but not for long."

"Miles never paid close attention," Daisy said, aching to the marrow of her bones. "It wasn't his fault. He didn't *want* to pay close attention. He wasn't even courting me. Regina burst into the room, and I instinctively claimed Belle as mine. After that, things happened so quickly that there wasn't time for objective reasoning."

"*Au contraire*, darling, there's been plenty of time. If your Miles wanted to face the truth about Belle's parentage, he had all last night to do it. But he never cottoned on to reality—which suggests he didn't allow himself to think about reality. He took the excuse to marry you and ran with it. Frankly, I would have done the same."

Daisy gave him a watery smile. "Thank you."

"I suppose Belle is your half-sister?" His voice was very kind.

She nodded. "My father has refused to take responsibility for her. I've decided to move to Brussels and live with your brother and Livie. My disastrous marriage can be annulled in my absence. I'll pretend that I'm widowed, and that Belle is my only child."

"You'd prefer a false widowhood to marrying me?" Frederick asked, not looking very hopeful.

She shook her head. "I couldn't."

"You really fell in love with him, didn't you?" His voice was curiously flat.

She shrugged. "I thought I did. It's astonishing how fast infatuation withers when a husband is chastising you for being a liar." Daisy's eyes filled with tears. "He says I trapped him in marriage because I fancied myself in love, and oh, Frederick, I think he's right. And he said I was stupid to run to him for help, and I suppose I was."

Frederick growled low in his chest. "He said you were stupid?"

"He said the idea of going to his house was stupid, but it's the same, isn't it? If you're wondering, the marriage isn't consummated, so it doesn't really matter. Those vows we spoke this morning can evaporate as quickly as they were spoken. He never meant them, anyway."

Frederick got up, walked across the room, and came back with two goblets of golden liqueur. "*Not* whiskey. A very ladylike Spanish wine that seems appropriate to celebration disunion."

Daisy took an unladylike swig and started coughing. "It's so sweet."

"I hate it, so it doesn't tempt me to drink over much," Frederick said. "Oates-Plagitt bought a case, hoping to prevent me from putting any further holes in my liver."

"I should have come to you instead of Miles," Daisy said miserably. She leaned sideways until she slumped against his shoulder.

Frederick wrapped an arm around her. "You know that our esteemed butler, Oates-Plagitt, is able to solve almost any problem, don't you?"

"Not this one: Miles hates me."

"He probably didn't like being lied to," Frederick said gently. "People don't."

"Oh for God's sake," Daisy cried, straightening up. "My father and mother lied to me for *years*, about everything: about why Livie was living with us, about where my father was living, about the existence of my many half-brothers and sisters!"

"*Many?*" Frederick repeated, obviously startled.

"I hadn't even gotten around to telling Miles that I wanted to adopt the other children," Daisy said, wiping tears from her cheeks. "He was busy shouting at me about my appalling lies."

Frederick was silent for a moment, and then he nudged her shoulder with his. "They were appalling, Daisy. You do see that, don't you? Miles married you thinking that he was saving you from a fate worse than death, but it turns out that you had simply decided to raise a child who wasn't your own and used him to get your way."

A sob tore its way out of Daisy's throat. "It sounds so awful, put like that."

"I know you didn't mean it as such." She felt something on her head, as if he dropped a kiss on her hair.

"I thought that I could never find another man who would contemplate marrying me and raising Belle as his own. Would you really have done that, Frederick?"

A silence, then: "For my sins, I'd probably have said yes to anything you asked, Daisy."

She rubbed her head against his shoulder. "My mother told me it was a mistake not to confess the truth before we married. But before this happened, he was indifferent, and I was so infatuated... He wouldn't have married me if I had told the truth."

"I'm not so sure about that."

"Can you please send your butler out to buy myself and my maid passage on the first boat leaving for Brussels? I can't be faced by all that despisement whenever I glimpse Miles in passing. Is despisement a word?"

Frederick shook his head. "No, but I see what you mean."

"I expect Regina will scoop him up. I expect she never bothers to lie, so she will make an excellent Lady Devin."

"She has no need to lie. She simply wields her opinions like a bludgeon. No one dares to contradict her."

Exhaustion weighed so heavily on Daisy that she could hardly keep her eyes open. "It's been the most wretched day," she said with a sigh. "Not precisely the wedding day I dreamed about when I was a little girl."

Frederick kissed her head again; this time she heard the small sound. "I suppose your imaginary groom was infatuated?"

"Desperate with love," Daisy confirmed. "I pictured myself taller and thinner. I would drift up the cathedral aisle, looking so beautiful that he would spring up in his eyes." She shook her head. "I was foolish then and foolish now."

"You are not a fool, but one of the most intelligent women I know," Frederick told her in a matter-of-fact tone. Before she could respond, he rolled her on her side and shifted so he could stretch out, leaving her wedged between him and the back of the sofa.

Daisy put her head on his shoulder. He smelled like whiskey and wood smoke, with just a touch of ink. "I feel very safe, tucked next to you. Do you suppose Belle feels safe in her basket?"

"She is safe in your arms," he said. "Go to sleep, Daisy. Everything is better after a nap."

"What are you reading?" she asked.

"*Glenarvon*, Lady Caroline's Lamb's new novel," Frederick said.

"I didn't like it. Did you know that Miles has never read a novel, not even one? Not even *Pride and Prejudice*, though everyone in polite society claims to have read it."

"That's a clear sign of future marital infelicity," Frederick said. "He has no respect for the fictional worlds most of us escape to in order to survive the real one. Why didn't you like *Glenarvon*? I'm tearing through it."

"The biographical aspect. She's not even trying to disguise a nasty portrait of Lord Byron as Lord Glenarvon."

"Personally, I'm enjoying reading about the corruption of a young, innocent bride, though Caroline hardly fits the bill."

"It's an absurd book. What about the fact that the heroine's infant brother is murdered and shows up alive later?"

"You're spoiling it! He's still dead to me," Frederick complained.

"Soon he'll be coming back from the dead. I suppose I'll be an innocent bride forever," Daisy said, hearing the ache in her own voice. "Not that I care much," she added. "But I don't like being shouted at. I'm impulsive and stupid and all the things he said, but I don't like shouting."

"You make decisions faster than the rest of us. You do have a tendency to lie to get your way, but you'll outgrow it. As you said, your mother and father lied to you for years, so you never had a good model in that respect."

She chuckled sleepily. "I left Miles a message saying that I wasn't in love with him any longer."

"Was that a lie?" Frederick asked softly.

She didn't answer.

He sighed and opened up his book again. Hopefully he could get to the end before Miles showed up.

Episode 111:
The Throne of Love

The Albany was a large brick building in Piccadilly, built for a viscount and divided into apartments for wealthy young men after his lordship realized he couldn't afford all that magnificence. Miles climbed from his carriage in front of the entrance, anger still setting his teeth on edge.

It felt as if all the corruption, unkindness, and sexual depravity he'd been forced to witness—and investigate—had come down to this: a man so vile that he refused to wear a condom, resulting in children whom he discarded like snagged silk stockings: imperfect, worthy of no notice, tossed aside to be mended by someone else.

By his long-suffering wife, Lady Wharton. Or by Miles's wife.

Daisy's father apparently didn't care that most of his children were considered a disgrace, degraded from the moment they breathed air, the sins of their father visited on their heads.

The entrance to the Albany clung to the trappings of an aristocratic home, though with a touch of self-consciousness, like a noblewoman fallen on hard times. The Aubusson rug was worn before the door, but numerous candles burned brightly, and the butler who advanced to meet Miles was properly attired in black with snowy white touches.

"I am Lord Devin," Miles said, pulling off his hat and gloves.

"It is a pleasure to welcome you to the Albany, your lordship," the man said with a deep bow. "My name is Mr. Guppy, and I've the pleasure of butlering for all seventy-three bachelor apartments. One of the very best has recent—"

"I'm married," Miles interrupted him. "And so, by the way, is Lord Wharton, so 'bachelor apartments' is something of a misnomer, is it not?"

"The famous poet, Lord Byron, also lives here, and he is married," Guppy said brightly. "Am I to take it that you'd like to pay Lord Wharton a visit, my lord? If you'll give me your card, I'll see if his lordship is receiving."

"No, you'll take me to his door on the double," Miles said, handing his greatcoat, hat, and gloves to a footman. Daisy was waiting at home. Waiting for him *in a towel.*

He'd been so enraged that it was only when he was driving away from the house that he abruptly realized that he'd made a ludicrous mistake. He'd been close to bedding the one woman whom he'd desired in years. Instead, he'd left her sitting on the bed in peach-cheeked perfection while fury swept him into a carriage.

When had anger and revulsion ever swayed him to this extent? He'd been unkind to her, too. Wretchedly unkind, and he felt ashamed of it.

He would send a note to Lord Paget resigning his post tomorrow morning. He'd had enough of the dissolute practices of the wealthy and mighty. The anger that was swilling in his gut wasn't due to his hasty marriage. It stemmed from countless hours spent listening to gentlemen with hard smiles explain away their crimes.

He wanted no more of it.

The only thing he wanted, in fact, was to return home and make peace with his wife. Because Daisy was terribly important to him. He hadn't realized how important until he was in a carriage bowling away from her.

"Here you are, my lord. Number sixty-nine, and you are lucky to find his lordship in on an evening. He's a night-owl, Lord Wharton."

Miles rapped on the door, thinking that he must have met Daisy's father at some point, though he had no memory of it. To the best of his recollection, his lordship did not attend his brother-in-law's treason trial.

The door was opened by a manservant. The gentleman who languidly rose from the couch seemed surprisingly youthful for a man in his sixties. Miles might actually have thought Lady Wharton was older than her husband, perhaps because worry and anger had worn on her spirit.

His lordship's silver hair had thinned significantly on the top of his head, so he had brushed the two sides up to meet in the middle like the ridgepole of a thatched roof. His cravat brushed his jowls in a fussy style worn by young men. Even worse, he was wearing fawn-colored, closely fitted pantaloons with an opening at the ankle.

"May I help you?" he inquired.

Miles jerked his head at the valet, who took himself away. "You may indeed help me," he said, walking into the apartment. The drawing room was pleasantly enough laid out, though a touch over-theatrical given its red velvet hangings and gilded wainscoting.

"Excuse me," Wharton said in a pained tone. "May I know who you are? If you are a bailiff—"

"I am your son-in-law," Miles said, wheeling about.

Wharton gasped, "No." He might have turned pale from shock, but no sign was visible since he wore a thick layer of face paint, his cheeks dusted with rouge.

"Yes," Miles said, walking close enough to confirm inadequately disguised syphilis scabs around the man's mouth. A beat of sadness went through him, not for the wretched Wharton, but for Daisy, who had lost her good regard for her father and was likely to lose him altogether in the near future.

"You must have forced my girl," Wharton said, his voice rising. "Daisy's too young to be married."

"She is over twenty."

He blinked at this clearly unwelcome information. "Did you elope with her?" he demanded, recovering.

"Do you care?"

"Of course I care! As she is mine, I may dispose of her. I've told her mother many a time that I won't allow her to marry below the nobility." Wharton's eyes rested disdainfully on Miles's hastily tied cravat.

"You're in luck," Miles said, seating himself. "I am Lord Devin. My claim to nobility stretches back to a close friend of Henry VIII."

Wharton squinted as if trying to place the name. Of course, he didn't spend much time fraternizing with polite society.

"I'm primarily known for my fortune," Miles said, solving the problem for him.

"Whoever you are, you married my daughter without asking for my permission," Wharton crabbed, his expression indicating that was a stupendous calamity. He sat down opposite Miles, plucking at his pantaloons to make certain that the openings at his ankles didn't bunch up.

"As I said, I married her this morning."

"I had no chance to walk my only daughter down the aisle!" Lord Wharton cried with a fiery emphasis that suggested his emotions could only be alleviated by money.

Only daughter?

Miles felt like a shark closing in on a mackerel. "I married Daisy after she arrived on my doorstep with a baby," he said, crossing his arms over his chest.

"Balderdash!" her father spat. "My daughter is as innocent as the driven snow. Her mother would allow no less. Besides, she's not exactly the kind of woman who has men sniffing at her heels, is she?"

Miles suddenly realized that while he had idly contemplated challenging his father-in-law to a duel, at this moment he would prefer to strangle him. Strangling felt more satisfying than leveling a rapier. "Your daughter is a beautiful, charming woman who had a circle of men at her feet before marrying me," he said through clenched teeth.

"You must be infatuated," Wharton said with a crack of laughter.

Seized by rage, Miles lunged out of his chair, twisting his father-in-law's neckcloth and jerking him to his feet. "You will *never* speak of my wife again in such an insolent manner."

"My cravat!" Wharton squawked, pulling away. Miles let him go. "The *Trone d'Amour* took me well over an hour to perfect."

"Throne of love?" Miles asked. "Ironic."

Wharton ignored him, running to a glass on the opposite wall. "Ruined," he moaned. "Ruined." He soothed the crushed folds of starched silk as if he were patting an outraged cat.

"Oh, for God's sake," Miles said, dropping back into his chair.

Wharton's manservant carried in two glasses of sherry on a silver tray. He registered the state of his master's attire with a yelp.

"Just so," Wharton said mournfully. "I shall be *very* late to the club this evening, Manning. Please send a message to Chesney."

Apparently too shaken to offer sherry, the valet set down his tray and left.

His lordship strolled back across the room and seated himself, shaking his pantaloons again before he looked at Miles with a peevish expression. Not a drop of fear, Miles noticed. Daisy's plucky nature had apparently been inherited along with her hair color.

"So you married my daughter," Wharton stated. "I am shocked, sir. *Shocked.* In my day, we didn't behave with such raffish haste."

"Really?" Miles said genially. "I was under the distinct impression that you eloped with Daisy's mother. Aren't you going to ask anything further about the baby?"

"My daughter's by-blow? I see nothing to discuss." He narrowed his eyes. "Unless *you* took her precious virginity, a woman's greatest gift to her husband."

"I did not."

"Then I suspect you hope for a larger dowry under the circumstances, but you shan't get it from me. You could try her mother. I don't mind telling you that Lady Wharton is a terrible nipcheese. Her behavior throughout our marriage has been dishonorable and unprincipled. I say that only to you, since you're a family member."

"Actually, I'd describe you as 'dishonorable and unprincipled,'" Miles remarked.

"Don't tell me the bailiffs have been after you already, and you only married Daisy this morning!" Wharton said, straightening and looking truly indignant.

"They have not."

"They will," he sighed. "You can't imagine how persistent those fellows are. The tailor who made these pantaloons proved himself a hawk." He leveled a finger at Miles. "Don't pay him. He doesn't deserve it."

"I shan't," Miles said. He was beginning—despite himself—to feel a touch of wry amusement. "What I shall do is care for your offspring. I have the feeling the child's mother first applied to you for help."

Wharton let out a loud cry, throwing his hands into the air. "Is there no stop to the lunacy to which a gentleman is subjected? The child is surely not mine, and I know nothing of it. If you wish, you may bankrupt yourself supporting the tarnished progeny of brothel dwellers. It is not for me to say. But I have no part in that girl's conception!"

"How did you know that the child was female?" Miles inquired. "I didn't say."

Wharton scowled. "I'd admit that a French vixen, Hortense, thought to charge me with the child's care since the woman was determined to return to her own country. 'Tis nothing to do with me! Her profession is such that she ought to have guarded against this inevitability."

Miles rose to his feet. "Be prudent with that frown, Lord Wharton. The wrinkles may prove permanent."

"Out," Daisy's father cried, leaping to his feet. "Have you not insulted me enough? Making your way into my presence pretending to be a bailiff, and accosting me with news of an ill-begotten brat who is no business of mine?"

Wharton had no conscience, no morals, and no concern for his children. To inflict his presence on Belle would be folly; Miles was caught by sincere regret that Daisy had grown up with this cold fish for a father.

"In six months I intend to announce that a cousin of yours, born on the wrong side of the blanket, has died in India, leaving his legitimately born child in your care. In turn, you will allot Belle to my guardianship."

"Oh, I will, will I?"

"From this day forward you will have no contact with either of your daughters. If you visit brothels in the future, you will wear a condom."

"My behavior is none of your business!" Lord Wharton blustered.

Miles narrowed his eyes and waited.

Wharton shrugged. "As it happens, this, ah, gentleman's complaint has curtailed my romantic life. You may have married Daisy—and I still want to see the marriage certificate—but you've no right to order me about!"

"I could remove you from this snug apartment as easily as a mouse is evicted from its hole," Miles said contemptuously. "Or I could pay off those bailiffs, ensuring that my wretched father-in-law doesn't embarrass his daughters by being hounded before the courts or sent to debtor's prison."

A charged silence followed.

"I suppose you shall have your way," Lord Wharton said heavily. "I remember who you are now. The guardian of morality in the House of Lords, aren't you? You hounded the poor Earl of Debbleton for the grave crime of owning his own theater."

"He was forcing young women from the country to engage in sexual acts on his stage."

"Rubbish! They were well paid—and well satisfied. Debbleton is always generous. The men in my club took it amiss, I don't mind telling you. I don't suppose you could neglect to announce this wedding in the paper? I'd rather not be associated with you."

"An announcement of my marriage has already been sent to *The Times*. While I am proud to have married your daughter, I have no more wish to be connected with you than you to me. I certainly don't give a damn about the opinion of the hellhounds belonging to whatever club invited you to join." He headed for the door.

"Hypocrite. You're a hypocrite and a liar," Lord Wharton spat.

Miles turned. "Would you care to elaborate?"

"You? With your infamous propensity for Russian dancers? You dare to wield a holier-than-thou attitude toward Lord Debbleton? Do you think that those dancers were well paid? Well-treated? From Russia rather than the countryside? Rumor has it you paid for the attentions of any number of strumpets and only later began judging others for doing the same."

Miles's jaw tightened. His hand landed on the rapier slung on his hip—and froze. The man wasn't entirely wrong.

"Who's to say that you don't have the odd bastard floating around London?" Wharton hissed.

"I always used a French letter, for my protection and that of the woman in question."

His father-in-law's mouth twisted, but he kept silent.

"If I ever hear that you recovered from your ailment sufficiently to enter a brothel, there'll be no money from that point," Miles stated. "No matter whether you're dragged off to debtor's prison or not."

"My doctor seems fairly certain that I won't live to see the new year," Wharton said abruptly. "The pox has spread, though it isn't visible."

"Daisy will be sorry to hear that."

"She always chattered too much for my taste, but she's a good lass, nothing like her mother. I suppose you'll take care of her?"

"My wife will always be safe with me. As will your other daughter, Belle."

"That mopsie is not—" Lord Wharton broke off at the look in Miles's eyes. "*Likely* not mine," he amended.

"Even though she has your hair and your daughter's face? Let me know when you're at death's door and I'll bring Daisy to say goodbye," Miles said. "You owe her that."

Then he left, closing the door quietly behind him.

Episode 112:
Yes, She's Gone

When Hobbs opened the door to the house, Miles read his face before he said a word. "My wife left, didn't she?" He stripped off his outer garments as the butler babbled about the baby, nappies, and rusks. At least Daisy remembered to take some food. "Where did she go?"

"I do not know, your lordship," Hobbs said, wringing his hands. "Her ladyship insisted on taking a hackney carriage."

"Next time, tell a groom to jump on the back," Miles said. "Or summon two hackneys and order the second to follow her."

"Next time?" Hobbs repeated. "My lord, you don't understand! Lady Devin has left you. She talked—" He stopped and wiped his brow. "The truth of the matter is that she talked of annulling the marriage."

"I'll bring her back," Miles said.

And consummate that marriage, so annulment isn't an option, he added silently.

"She left you a letter in her bedchamber."

"Right. Keep the carriage at the curb. I'll go after her."

"I have interviews with nannies, my lord. Should I—"

"Of course!" Miles interrupted. "Find us a good one, Hobbs."

He bounded up the steps, feeling oddly light. His wife—his beloved wife—was rightly furious at him. Not for the last time. He had called her a liar, which was cruel but perhaps fair. Yet his own sins were far greater.

She loved him. She would forgive him.

Though when he was staring down at her letter, his certainty wavered. Daisy had obviously been deeply unhappy when she wrote the note; there were blurred spots on the sheet, as if tears had fallen there. Miles rubbed them with his thumb, as if he could wipe away her sorrow.

The sorrow *he* had stupidly caused.

In truth, he didn't give a damn why they got married. He would never give away Belle. In fact, he felt a distinct pang of alarm at the fact that Daisy was running around the city with their daughter in a basket once again. At least this time a maid was in attendance.

"I don't want to remain married to you. I can't live with a husband who despises me."

That was pretty straightforward. He'd been a sanctimonious ass. His reaction had sprung from base rage instead of heartfelt truth. Now that he'd calmed down, it was inconceivable to him that he had stormed out of the room like a child in a tantrum.

Leaving her there, vulnerable and rejected.

Of course she'd left him.

He couldn't read the next line because tears had blurred the ink—something about a laundry basket—but the gist was clear enough: she didn't feel worthwhile enough to marry him. A sour taste rose up his throat.

Worthwhile? She was innocent and good, interested only in saving her sister from an orphanage, whereas in contrast he had nothing to be righteous about. Nothing.

Lord Wharton's scorn wasn't misplaced: even given that he stayed within the bounds of acceptable gentlemanly behavior, that didn't change the unethical nature of his actions.

"Belle wouldn't have been mine any longer."

Also true. Had Daisy immediately disclosed Belle's fatherhood after arriving at his house, he would have found Wharton and forced him to accept his responsibilities. Not that Belle would have been dispatched to an orphanage, but likely to a good woman in the country. That was the fate of most infants born on the wrong side of the blanket, at least if they were fathered by men with a conscience. Daisy would have been unlikely to see Belle again.

Yet Miles had flown Belle into the air the way he had his sisters. He had walked the floor all night long, the wailing child clinging to him. Around six in the morning, Belle had looked at him with drenched blue eyes and then, with a shuddering sigh, tucked her head into the curve of his shoulder.

He claimed not to believe in love at first sight, but he was already in love with his daughter.

"I want an annulment."

No. His whole body recoiled at the thought.

He wasn't only in love with Belle. He had seen Daisy at the masquerade and gone directly to her side. He had looked for her everywhere, even after Lady Wharton declined his proposal. He may have refused to acknowledge his emotions, but his actions spoke for themselves.

He wanted to give his wife the world—but not an annulment. Never that. He raked his fingers through his hair, thinking hard about what to do next.

Lady Wharton would be unsympathetic, so Daisy had surely gone to Frederick—who was desperately in love with her.

Miles had never considered himself a possessive man; jealousy suggested an unbecoming level of sentiment. But thinking about Daisy in distress, fleeing to Frederick?

He took a deep breath. Then he threw himself back down the stairs and out the door before Hobbs could produce his greatcoat. A half hour later he sprang from his carriage in front of a townhouse so old that it leaned over the street like an aging spinster who'd misplaced her cane.

"Good afternoon, Oates-Plagitt," he said, greeting the butler.

"Good afternoon, Lord Devin. We have been expecting you. Your wife is in the library." Rather than escort him, Oates-Plagitt stepped back and gestured toward a huge oak door.

"Where is Belle?"

The butler smiled. "She has charmed everyone below stairs and is currently taking a nap in the arms of our cook, who has announced that supper will be delayed."

Miles entered the library silently, his eyes going directly to the sofa. Daisy was lying on her side, cozied up against Frederick's shoulder, rumpled hair spilling over his chest. Frederick's arm was wrapped around her, anchoring her against his side.

Jealousy gnawed at Miles's gut. His teeth clenched as he fought a wave of anger and betrayal. Daisy was *his*. She had vowed—only this morning—to be his.

Except he had left her first.

He had walked out, leaving her unclothed and unloved.

"Shouldn't you be wearing a fool's cap?" Frederick asked in a hushed voice, glancing up from his book. "I haven't got around to trimming one with diamonds, but for you, I could make an effort."

Miles walked over and looked down at the two of them. Daisy was pale with exhaustion, her golden lashes dark against her cheeks. The way her hand clung to Frederick's lapel sent a piercing ache through his heart that hurt as much as the fact that she was lying beside another man.

"Fool's cap?" he muttered, collecting himself enough to remember the long-ago conversation in the ballroom. "I suppose so."

Frederick lay his open book down on his stomach. "I'm not sure a hat would sufficiently signal your idiocy, given that you apparently concluded that this darling girl had a virgin birth."

Miles sat down opposite them. "May I please take my wife home?"

"No," Frederick said pleasantly enough. "Just how did you think that Daisy managed to carry a child for nine months without you or anyone else noticing? Didn't you scold her for riding too fast in Hyde Park—during the period when she would presumably have been heavy with child?"

"She said Belle was hers. I believed her." His voice came out gritty with emotion. Obviously, he was an idiot.

"You *wanted* to believe her. There's a difference."

Miles absorbed that, nodding. "Please stop embracing my wife."

Frederick didn't move a hair. "I suppose your pride stung when you found her gone. But I gather you left first, rashly dashing out of the house to attack her buffoon of a father. And yet you accused Daisy of impulsivity? Leave her alone. She's exhausted."

Despite himself, Miles's hands curled into fists. "Frederick."

"Exhausted," Frederick repeated.

"I will carry her to the carriage." His words grated like rocks on a dry riverbed.

"No, you will carry your daughter after Daisy wakes up." Frederick squinted at him. "Do you have any bloody idea how lucky you are?"

"I am learning."

"She wants you." The aching tone in his voice spoke for itself. "If you're not fool enough to drive her away again, you'll keep her forever, because she's loyal, even to a drunken sod like me."

"I won't." It was a vow that came from the heart, unlike those he had spoken that morning.

"Then sit down and let her sleep." Frederick picked up his book.

The only sound in the room was the popping of sparks in the fireplace and the gentle swish of Frederick's pages turning. From where he sat, Miles could see a pale wash of Daisy's hair. It wasn't precisely moonlit silver; pale straw would be a better comparison, with a few strands of amber woven here or there. As he sat, her cheeks gradually flushed from sleep and her hand relaxed, setting free Frederick's lapel and lying flat against his chest.

His chest.

Not Miles's chest.

Never again, he told himself silently.

He had betrayed their marriage by storming out in a rage. His punishment was to see her pressed close to another man, a man to whom she'd fled for comfort.

Her husband should be comforting her. Hell, her husband should have made sure that his wife wouldn't run away in a hackney cab. The truth slowly dawned on Miles. He didn't know how to *be* a husband, and he'd failed at the task in a matter of hours.

His parents had died years ago, and searching his memory didn't help. Were they loving toward each other? Kind? He had no idea, though five children suggested that if nothing else, they liked each other better than Daisy's parents did.

Still, he remembered his father's burst of anger after his youngest sister was born; even at thirteen years old, he had understood that his father wanted a second boy. A spare heir, in case his only son died.

The work Miles did at the House of Lords had consolidated his belief that marriage was a matter of money and birth. Heirs were important. Spare heirs were also important. Emotions should be corralled outside of the house, and definitely outside the marital bed.

He had tried to protect himself by labeling Daisy as impulsive, but so was he. He'd called her foolish, but so was he. Strong-willed? So was he. He could picture himself twenty or thirty years from now, arguing with his beautiful wife at the breakfast table. The picture wasn't quite right, so he added Belle, cheerful but naughty. And then two more children with Daisy's eyes.

If he could talk her into staying married to him.

"Oh, for God's sake," Frederick muttered.

Miles opened his eyes.

Frederick waved his book in the air. "Don't bother reading this absurd piece of drivel." He tossed it to the carpet and then gently slid away from Daisy, who didn't stir. As Miles watched, Frederick strode across the room and snatched up the brandy decanter.

"Well, go on," he said, heading for the door.

Miles rose. "Wake her?"

Frederick rolled his eyes. "Your wife. My couch. I'll warn everyone that you are finally consummating your marriage and not a minute too soon."

"I am *not* consummating my marriage on your couch!"

"I admit to being grateful to hear it," Frederick said. "Stop being an ass, Miles."

"I will."

Episode 113: The Truth Can be More Painful than Lies

Daisy woke up slowly. Her cheek was crushed against a strong male shoulder. She dimly remembered going to sleep next to Frederick, but this was not Frederick. After only a few hours of marriage, she already recognized her husband's particular mix of spice and clean linen.

Miles slept like a cat, quiet and self-possessed. One of his arms clamped her to his side and the other curved around her waist. He looked...

He looked male and satisfied and rather pleased with himself.

Which was absurd, since his bride had left him, planning to move abroad.

While she was still thinking about his expression, his long eyelashes fluttered. They looked black from afar, but this close they were thick and brown, like mink fur. Sculpted cheekbones, deep bottom lip, strong chin... His beauty registered like a thump of her heart.

If only—*if only*—she felt equal to him. If she were Regina, but kinder. The daughter of a duke, slim, beautiful, always neat, never impulsive.

"Your expression is so bleak," he said, focusing on her face.

How did he imagine she would look? Happy to see him?

Daisy lifted the arm that anchored her to his side and pushed it away. "This has been a horrible day. The wedding, remember? Followed by both husband and wife realizing that they had made a mistake."

"I didn't realize that," he said.

The ache in her chest felt sharp, as if a claw had reached into her body and pierced her heart. "Actually, you said precisely that. Why are you here, Miles? Our marriage, such as it is, is over." Her voice sounded ragged, almost timid. She had to pull herself together and be the strong, independent woman Belle deserved. "I left you."

"Actually, I left you."

"That too." Somehow their feet had entangled, their thighs pressed together. Daisy pulled her legs away from his, wrenching her gown down until it covered her ankles. "Would you please rise so that I can get up?"

Miles shook his head. "No. I didn't mean to leave you permanently. You're my wife."

"Not legally," she pointed out.

"I'm sorry that I left before making love to you. I was an ass."

"You were," she agreed, not in a mood to prevaricate.

"Then allow me to apologize properly."

Given the flare of hunger in Miles's eyes, Daisy knew exactly what he intended before his head lowered. Her mouth instinctively opened to his. His kiss was raw and sexual, making the ache in her chest intensify as she fought his erotic pull.

She couldn't allow Miles to make love to her, not only because it would make their marriage legal, but because a true marriage to him would break her heart into even smaller pieces.

"We belong together," he whispered, drawing back.

"No," she said, shaking her head. Somehow, while sleeping, her thoughts had moved from chaotic despair to concrete logic. "We desire each other, but that's not enough. Lust doesn't prevent people from behaving horribly toward each other. We have that, but it's all we have." Thankfully, her voice didn't sound as breathless as she felt. "I can't control how you feel about me, but I can control how much your disrespect affects me. *And* how much it affects Belle."

He opened her mouth, but she shook her head again. "I know I deserve your insults. I lied to you. I did go to your house, rather than to Frederick's, because I considered myself in love with you. I did *not* plan to lure you into marriage. I honestly thought you had likely fathered children and could hide Belle amongst them. But I did lie to you about her parentage. I apologize for that falsehood, Miles. I am truly sorry that my stupid behavior changed your life so drastically."

His brows pulled together, his eyes darkening. Just like that, his face transformed from the countenance of a patrician highborn lord to that of a regular human. Daisy's heart thumped again. She adored her scowling, lustful husband far more than the gentleman she'd initially fallen in love with, the man with sculpted cheekbones and elegant clothing.

"Luckily, we aren't yet truly married," she continued, clearing her throat. "Not legally. There's time for both of us to reconsider this rash decision. I have rethought it. You may not have had the time, but I am certain you agree with me. Inside, you agree with me."

"We have more than desire," Miles said, his frown deepening. "There's Belle, for one thing."

Daisy scowled back at him. "Belle is mine."

"She's mine as well. You gave her to me."

"Nonsense. You called her a 'prostitute's get.' Do you really think that I should allow you to father her after that insult?"

His face was a complicated mix of regret and anger. "I apologize wholeheartedly for that insult. I spoke in anger, and I will never say anything like that about Belle ever again. She *is* yours. I understand that."

"Our marriage was a farce, easily annulled. I'm taking Belle, *my* daughter, to Brussels." She pushed back against the couch. "Please don't make me clamber over you."

"We have more between us than Belle," Miles said stubbornly.

"Back to lust." Daisy sighed. "Our vows were meaningless. I can't stay married to you."

"Why not?"

She took a deep breath and then just told him the truth. "Underneath the desire, you despise me. You probably always considered me too young and impulsive, but after lying to you and forcing you into marriage? There's no way forward for us, Miles. I can't do it." Despite herself, her voice splintered, but she reached for control again.

"Daisy—"

"Move aside!" She pushed his arm, and he drew back. She inelegantly scrambled over him to get off the couch and stand up. She must look a sight. Her dress was rumpled, and heavy coils of hair had fallen down her back.

But that was just as well. Miles might as well see her for the last time without the veneer of fine dressing: short, ungraceful, messy, so much *less* than he was.

Her head hurt. And her heart hurt.

He rose, and she turned to face him rather than fleeing the room because he deserved an explanation; news of the annulment would soon be the talk of all society. Once she left for the continent, he would be left to brave the scandal.

Her breath hitched when their eyes met, but she forced herself to get the words out. "After the ceremony this morning, I asked you not to make me feel unlovable." She paused to take a breath because it felt as if her throat were tightening, and her voice had a humiliating wobble.

"I apologize," Miles said. "I never wanted to hurt you, Daisy."

She believed him. He was a perfect gentleman, after all. He would never want to hurt her feelings—or any other woman's.

Daisy waved her hand. "Perhaps you shouldn't have shared your opinion of me on our wedding day."

He opened his mouth, but she shook her head.

"Yet I would have learned how you felt the first time we argued. I can't do it, Miles. I thought I could marry someone who didn't love me, and that my love would be enough for both of us. I was wrong." Her hands twisted together. "You should marry someone you respect."

"I do respect you."

She sighed. "You never wanted to marry *me*, did you? You never courted me. In fact, when I coupled you and Frederick as my suitors, you actually paled. Your first proposal occurred after my gown fell apart, and your second because I brought a baby to your house. Neither is a solid foundation for a marriage."

"Is it my turn to speak?"

Daisy shook her head. "Look me in the eyes and tell me that you didn't decide I was too foolish and impulsive to be your wife. That you didn't plan to find a wife who was well-groomed and eager to discuss political events rather than read scandalous novels. That there wasn't a part of you that was glad when my mother refused your proposal. That part of you didn't rage when Regina walked into your room, and I blurted out that the baby was mine ... and you realized that you were trapped."

Miles opened his mouth—and then closed it.

It felt as if the air thickened during his painful silence.

"All those things are true."

Episode 114:
The Right Kind of Wife

The pain in Daisy's heart was so profound that she could hardly draw breath. She'd known how Miles felt before he confirmed it, and most of society probably agreed with his judgment. So why did it feel as if she'd taken a blow to the gut?

Because it was *his* opinion. Miles was important to her, despite her attempts to convince herself otherwise. It hurt to look at him, so she concentrated on shaking out her skirts, her hands trembling. "Thank you for your honesty. If you'll excuse me—"

His voice rumbled from his chest. "None of those things mattered. I did think you were impulsive and too young. I was furious that you lied to me. But none of that matters."

Daisy looked down at the hand curled around her upper arm. "I have to leave, Miles."

"Did you ever wonder why you kept running into me during the Season, given that Clementine is engaged and my younger sisters are living in Bath? I had no reason to attend society's events, yet I went to any event where I thought you might appear. I looked for *you* everywhere I went."

"No, you were looking for a wife," she reminded him. "Everyone knew that. The—the right kind of wife. Not me. You scarcely danced with me." The air in her lungs felt heated. "That's enough," she said, spinning around and heading for the door. "I trust you can arrange for the annulment in my absence."

"I refuse."

Hand on the door, Daisy looked over her shoulder. Miles was wearing a scowl so black that a nervous person would run blubbering from the room. She squared her shoulders and turned around fully. "You have no choice. This marriage is not yet legal."

"Do you know what I think about, seeing you against the wall like that?"

"This isn't a wall. It's a door."

"The night the back of your gown fell to the floor. You were fearless while many women would have gibbered in terror and embarrassment. Yes, I desired you. But I was also so *proud* of you. Proud to even know you. I would have told you the next day, but your mother made it clear that I should stay away from you. Frankly, I felt the same about your escapade in the Tower."

Daisy felt behind her for the latch. "Nonsense. You've repeatedly chastised me for that. Repeatedly!"

"I felt proud," he said flatly. "Angry because you might have got into trouble by foxing the guards at the Tower of London, but also awed. You managed to smuggle in a *file*, which hadn't been done since the 1500s."

"But you said—"

"I didn't want to feel that way. Why should I be proud of a girl who makes me ache with desire at the mere sight of her lips? Who laughs at me and pokes fun and prefers to spend her time with Frederick? Who not only didn't faint after her gown fell apart, but looked at me with aching desire in her eyes?"

"Pride implies ownership," Daisy observed. "You were not my suitor nor even my friend."

"I was the man who was falling in love with you. One of many."

Her mouth fell open, gracelessly. She couldn't force out a word.

Miles walked toward her slowly. "I am in love with you, Daisy. I considered you mine long before your dress fell off, though I didn't allow myself to acknowledge the fact. You described yourself walking to my house like a homing pigeon? I saw you at that damned masquerade and went to you like the homing pigeon's mate."

Daisy's heart felt as if it was beating in her mouth. "But you were trying to ... to find a woman at Rothingale's house."

He shook his head. "No. I was about to leave when I caught sight of your hair."

"Because you wanted to *buy* me," Daisy pointed out. She didn't try to suppress the jaundiced edge in her voice.

Surprisingly, he smiled. "I don't suppose you respect my decision to accept Rothingale's invitation? He did warn me, earlier in the day, that the attendees would be high-flyers. Strumpets," he clarified.

"No, I do not respect that decision," she said, fuming. She crossed her arms over her chest. "I attended that vulgar event due to a misunderstanding, but you went there looking to hire a woman for the night. Who could possibly respect *that?*"

His hand curled around her cheek. "We won't respect every decision our spouse has made or will make, darling. We'll just have to apologize for our mistakes. I promise I will never attend anything like that masquerade again. I will never again consider sleeping with a woman other than my wife. I chastised you for fibbing, as if I hadn't done far worse. I deserve your disdain."

"I stole your ability to marry another woman," Daisy pointed out.

He laughed. "Do you know how close Cropley, that idiot suitor of yours, came to being cut into small pieces for having the presumption to kiss you?"

She blinked. "Really?"

"You think I'm civilized? I'm not. You left my bed, and I found you an hour later sleeping next to another man. If Frederick wasn't who he is, I would have wrenched him out of your embrace and killed him. I've always prided myself on civility, so it's been a terrific shock to discover my barbaric instincts. It turns out that I'm ruthless, ungentlemanly, and thoroughly uncivilized. If you *ever* curl up next to Frederick again, I'll slay him."

"You wouldn't. He's your friend. Your best man!"

"Dead," Miles said with conviction. "He wants to steal the most important person in my life. He would give anything to marry you."

Daisy stared at him. Miles's voice was always deep, but now it had lowered to a masculine growl that his acquaintances in the House of Lords wouldn't have recognized. His elegant features had taken on a ruggedness that eclipsed the composure he generally displayed to the world.

A disconcerting flicker of heat made itself known in her belly.

"You told me that you were rarely homicidal," she pointed out.

"It's true ... except where you're concerned. That said, I can control myself. I didn't kill your father, though I was tempted."

"My father." Daisy drew in a sharp breath. "What happened with my father? I refuse to give Belle up, no matter what either of you say."

"I promised to pay off his debts. He will stay out of brothels from now on. After his many-times-removed cousin dies in India, he will relinquish guardianship of Belle to us."

"If I move to Belgium, no one will ever guess that she's not my daughter," Daisy said, feeling as if she were grasping at a straw to try to stay above water.

His eyes narrowed. "Belle is *my* daughter too."

"Nonsense," she said, tossing her head. More curls promptly fell down her back.

"Do you think that I would walk the floor all night with just any screaming child?"

Daisy opened her mouth, but Miles interrupted. "My turn to speak. I fell in love with your half-sister the first time Belle graced me with her adorably beaming smile. I was in a rage when I threatened to give her to your father. And I was exhausted. I said things I didn't mean and that shame me to remember them."

"Hobbs told me you have that tendency," Daisy said slowly.

"When I'm tired, I say things *impulsively. Irrationally.*" He stopped and looked at her expectantly.

"Oh."

"I also behave irrationally, slamming out of the house and leaving my naked wife on our bed. I try not to make the same mistake twice. I won't do it again."

"You won't?" Daisy had that dizzy feeling again, as if she'd been swept into a hurricane.

"We won't leave the bedroom for three days." His eyes were alight with raw hunger.

"No." She couldn't believe what she was hearing. Miles was saying things that she hadn't even dared to imagine. About her.

About... her.

"You ought to disdain me for my mistakes," he said, missing her point. "I'm irrational and irresponsible, and I stupidly dashed off to scold your father. I'm an idiot. Please forgive me." His voice ached with emotion as a big hand reached out to cradle her cheek.

"I forgive you," Daisy said. "But..."

"But?"

"I'm not sure that I want to remain married to you. It's not merely because I forced you to marry me," she said, bumbling into an explanation. "It all happened so fast that I'm not sure that I—"

"You love me," Miles interrupted.

"Well, I was infatuated," Daisy said awkwardly.

"No, you love me."

She cleared her throat. "Be that as it may, I'm not sure I want to be your wife. If we consummated the marriage, it would complicate annulment."

"Everyone in London knows we're married." He braced his hands on the door on either side of her, his eyes fixed on her face. "Frederick told me to consummate our marriage on his couch."

Daisy shuddered. "Ew!"

One side of his mouth eased into a reluctant smile. "He was grateful when I declined. My point is that it's too late to change your mind."

"I disagree," Daisy argued. "This is a huge decision, and I rushed you into it."

"Actually, I rushed you into it," Miles said. "I announced that we had to marry immediately. I could have suggested a ceremony in a week or a month. Belle might have been sent to the country, and we could have married ceremoniously in the cathedral with hundreds in attendance, and no baby to complicate the picture."

"Oh."

Daisy slowly let his words filter into her mind.

Into her heart.

"I was determined to marry you," Miles said. "The moment I saw an opportunity, I proclaimed that it would happen the very next day."

"There was no real reason for the rush, was there?" Daisy asked.

"None other than my desperation to get my ring on your finger." His voice wasn't rumbling any longer; it was warm and tender. He leaned closer and brushed his lips over her forehead.

Daisy had never felt more confused in her life.

"You didn't force me to marry you. If any other woman had strolled into my room with a baby, I would have offered help and sent her away. But you? The moment you walked in with a tiny replica of yourself, the only thing I could think was that I had to make you mine, whether some other man fathered your baby or no."

Daisy had a sinking feeling that his smile could convince her of anything. "I should see how Belle is doing." She felt behind her for the latch once again.

"I will court you," Miles said huskily. He bent his head and nipped her bottom lip. When she opened her mouth, his tongue met hers.

She dropped the latch and swayed toward him as his arms wrapped around her. When he was kissing her, she didn't feel like a bag of laundry; her body felt plush and right, designed to press against his hard contours.

They kissed until Daisy felt as if her body blazed with heat, as if a sheet of fire roared over her. Miles finally pulled back, looking at her with aching hunger.

"Desire is not enough for marriage," she blurted out shakily.

After another devouring kiss, he said, "Just so you know, Daisy, this is not garden-variety desire. I have never felt this out-of-control while kissing any woman. Ever." One of his hands roamed down her back and curved around her bottom before sliding up to her waist. "I am obsessed with your arse."

"One of my lovable parts?" she asked crossly. "That hurt my feelings."

His eyes crinkled, and with a jolt she realized that he was smiling. "What do you think about my arse?"

Daisy gaped at him. She was already flushed, but she grew even redder. "I—"

"Because once I got into the carriage and stopped being so *impulsive*, I remembered that you like my burly muscle. You can explore every part of me when we get home. Hopefully you'll find some of my parts lovable."

"Miles." Daisy protested, trying to pull together the tattered remains of her conviction.

He paused, looking into her eyes. His hands tightened on her waist. "You mean it, don't you?"

She nodded. "I have Belle. I'm not merely responsible for myself. I'm only now realizing how much my father's disinterest and estrangement from the family affected me as a child and as a woman. If you stormed out of the house in an argument...It wouldn't be good for Belle."

Miles's hands eased, and he brushed a kiss on her lips. A nuzzling kiss, an affectionate kiss, a kiss that seeped into the lonely parts of her heart. "I agree. Mind you, that goes for you as well. No jumping into a hackney cab and leaving me behind."

Daisy bit her lip. "That's just it, Miles. Perhaps we're too combustible."

"If we love each other, it won't matter. We won't consummate the marriage until we're both sure of that," Miles said.

His smile widened. "Until you beg me."

Episode 115:
The Campaign

The tightness in Daisy's chest unfurled a little, but she was still terrified. "I can't make a rash mistake," she found herself saying. "What if you decide you no longer like me, the way you did before?"

"When?"

"When what?"

"When did I stop liking you? I have always liked you."

"Not true. You thought I was a pain in the arse," Daisy told him. "Then you did like me, a bit. You thought I was funny, at least. After the proposal that my mother didn't tell me about, you looked at me with disdain. And disinterest." She swallowed. "I couldn't get you to laugh at all."

"Your mother told me that I couldn't marry you, and that I was a disgusting old man like your father."

"*What?*"

"Also that I should consider you only in an avuncular manner."

Anger surged to replace desire. "She had no right!"

"Avuncular regard wasn't a bad cover," he said musingly. "I was so angry that I kept looking for you everywhere, making a point of dancing with you and talking to you, all so that I could prove to your mother how disinterested I was. How avuncular."

"That's absurd!"

He nodded. "I was hurt. Oh, not by you, but by your mother's contempt."

"Why didn't you propose to *me*?"

"Because I thought I deserved her disparagement." His lips quirked into a wry smile. "We share that feeling. Didn't you say that you deserved my disdain? But you felt ashamed for the weighty crime of trying to save your adorable little sister. I deserved your scorn—and your mother's— because I did consort with Russian dancers. I *am* older than you, though only by seven years and not twenty."

"I don't care about that," Daisy said promptly.

"Good, because I'm a reformed man. Married. Faithful. Loyal to my dying day. In love with my wife."

The last words fell, heavy in the quiet room.

She opened her mouth, but he put a finger on her lips, a touch as soft as a snowflake. "Like any man in love, I mean to court the woman of my heart." The steady light in his eyes made Daisy's anxiety ease.

She'd never seen that expression on his face. In fact, she had the impression that no woman had seen it. All the same, fear rattled around in her gut. After all, in the past Miles had looked at her with passion ... and then the next evening with disinterest.

"As far as courting goes, it would be difficult to return to my mother's house and wait for invitations to drive in Hyde Park," she pointed out.

"We will take Belle to my country house, where I shall do my best to lure you into falling back in love with me. You shall sleep in your bedchamber and I in mine."

"You're going to woo me?" she asked shakily. "Even though we're already married?"

"Not legally," he reminded her.

"Do you mean with poetry?" She eyed him dubiously. "Flowers?"

Miles realized with a jolt that he had never actually courted a woman and wasn't certain how to do it. "Poetry might be a stretch," he confessed. "Perhaps I could find some verse in the library in the country. There are hundreds of volumes, so surely a sonnet or two can be found amongst them."

Her eyes widened. "Are there any novels?"

"I doubt it. The shelves are crammed full of books in Latin and Greek, thanks to scholarly ancestors."

Daisy's face fell. "I only read novels written in English."

Miles made a mental note to subscribe to every publishing house that sold novels. "The gardens are full of roses that I can toss at your feet."

"I prefer violets," she said, a smile growing in her eyes. "Roses are gaudy."

He nodded. "What else could I give you? Jewelry?"

She wrinkled her nose. "I'm not Lady Regina. She carries off diamonds with an air."

Miles had the idea that Regina draped herself with sparkling rocks in the hopes that men would overlook her sharp tongue. So far, it hadn't worked. "A kitten?" he asked, wracking his memory for appropriate gestures.

"No! You needn't give me anything. Truly."

Likely her father's disinterest, even contempt, had sunk into his wife's bones, so she needed to be wooed with the truth, not with diamonds or flowers. Miles cupped her face, cataloguing her lush features, her wide eyes, her shimmering hair. "You are beautiful, Daisy—but even more beautiful inside."

"I have heard that Lord Devin is remarkably eloquent in the House of Lords," she said, dimpling at him. "I am beginning to believe it."

"You're insightful, adventuresome, and intelligent. You have integrity and kindness. The generosity in your heart puts me to shame. You never considered allowing Belle to go to an orphanage, did you?"

She shook her head.

"Why wouldn't all of the bachelors in London fall in love with you? I had to marry you overnight, in case I lost you to one of them. They saw a woman gentle to the bone, with whom they could share a life full of laughter and love. Who was delightfully sensual but deeply loyal. Who would *love* them. That's one thing I learned from my position in the House of Lords. Most men in the peerage are unloved. Not to blame their wives: the fellows I encountered were fairly unlovable."

Daisy looked astonished. "You think all those things of me?"

"Obviously I need to prove it to you—so we'll share nothing more than kisses from now on. Until you beg me."

"I shan't beg you!" she said, turning pink.

An hour later, when Miles walked up the steps to his house, one hand held his daughter and the other his wife's hand.

Hobbs opened the door, stepping backward and bowing. "My lady, welcome back!"

Daisy smiled at him. "Your comment about my husband's irascibility when exhausted was helpful, Hobbs. Thank you."

Miles looked down at his wife. "I informed Hobbs that next time you run away, a footman should jump on the back of the hackney."

Daisy turned pink. "Miles!"

"I'm sure I'll do an impulsive, stupid thing or two in the next fifty years," he said, grinning at her. "You'll need to straighten me out."

"Hopefully not," Daisy said. She twinkled at Hobbs. "In that event, I'll turn a blind eye to a man in livery following me out the door."

"Just so, my lady," Hobbs said, not bothering to hide a grin.

"I'll be the man following you," Miles growled, dropping a kiss on her lips even though the butler and two footmen were watching. He turned to Hobbs. "Rather than spend the night in London, we shall leave for the country immediately. Our trunks have been sent ahead, haven't they?"

Hobbs nodded. "I'm happy to say that I have engaged a respectable nanny, who comes with the highest references. Nanny Plum is already in residence and prepared to travel with the household."

"Belle will travel in our carriage," Daisy said firmly.

The baby had slept the whole time they were in Frederick's house, making up for her sleepless night. Now she looked around at Hobbs, the footmen, Ada, and Miles. "Boo, boo, boo!"

"That's a new sound!" Daisy said, her eyes lighting up.

"Boo, boo," Belle repeated, and then, thoughtfully, "Moo."

Miles bent his head and kissed the baby soundly. "Moo to you, sweetheart."

Eight hours later, as the Devin carriages trundled up the drive to his lordship's country estate, Belle was sleeping in Miles's arms, and Daisy was curled up at his side.

He ran a light finger down his wife's nose, vowing to himself that his life's goal would be to make her happy. Raw desire struck him so desperately, so ferociously that he swallowed hard and reminded himself that courtship was next. He wanted Daisy to know in her bones how much he loved her before they made love.

In the last years, he had lost over and over, as criminal cases he had prepared were dismissed by the House of Lords, voted down by men more interested in protecting the reputation of their peers than seeing justice done.

Wooing Daisy meant more to him than any of those cases.

He refused to lose this time, which meant he had to be patient.

They climbed from the carriage in the dark, the courtyard lit by flickering gas lanterns and stars far above. His wife tipped her head back, staring at his house. Its tall, narrow windows glowed with golden light, showing glimpses of elaborately plastered ceilings.

"Welcome to Devin Manor," Miles said.

"It's so large," she breathed.

"King Henry VIII built the house as a residence for his eldest son, Henry, but the child only lived a few weeks. When His Majesty lost the house to my ancestor in a card game, it was said that the king purposefully threw his cards, as he wanted no reminders of Henry's death."

"A royal abode," Daisy said. "Goodness."

Miles handed Belle to Nanny Plum, picked up Daisy, and began to stride toward the door. "A fitting place for my queen to live."

"Miles! I told you that you mustn't pick me up like a bag of laundry!"

"Laundry?" he paused, letting the hand on her bottom tighten. "You don't feel like laundry to me." He dusted her lips with his. "You feel like my delectable, utterly desirable wife."

"You're the only man who ever called me that."

"Perhaps not to your face," Miles growled. "Believe me, your suitors thought it behind your back."

Daisy slung an arm around his neck. "I think you're delectable too," she whispered. "You don't mind that I can't keep my hair above my shoulders? That I don't take daily walks and eat nothing but rusks one day a week? That's what Lady Regina suggested."

"I love your hair. I don't want you to become slimmer. Your curves are everything to me. I want you to be who you are."

He set her gently onto the entry's flagstones.

"The Lady Devin," he said formally to his assembled household. He nodded toward Nanny Plum. "And Miss Belle Devin. My daughter."

Episode 116:
Courtship by Way of Violets

The next week was the happiest of Daisy's life. She and Miles took Belle with them everywhere: to the village in a pony cart, to the estate's tenant farmers in a carriage, to the trout river for fishing, and even into the kitchens and up to the attics.

Nothing Daisy knew of courting had prepared her for the delight of having a man stroll into her bedchamber in the morning and drop a handful of violets on her coverlet. And then squash all the blossoms because he'd rolled on top of them during a kiss.

At the end of the week, Miles brought Daisy and Belle to a clearing deep into the woods where the grass was a dark acid-green with a carpet of violets hanging over every blade.

"It's so lovely!" Daisy cried, looking about.

Miles shook out a blanket and set Belle down. She promptly reached for a handful of flowers and stuck them into her mouth.

"Don't eat those, Belle. They're better when candied," he told her, coming down on his knees and pulling a stem from her lips.

Belle frowned. "Boo-boo," she said, snatching another fat little fistful of crumpled flowers.

"You could teethe with this instead," Miles said enticingly, waving a silver rattle.

The baby grinned at him as she crammed the new bunch into her mouth, chomping down with all three teeth.

"I find it ominous that her smile grows bigger when she's being disobedient," Miles remarked, still trying to convince her to take the rattle.

Daisy sat down beside her family, her heart thumping as she watched them. Her husband was wearing an exquisite white linen shirt—but no coat or cravat, so she could see his corded neck. He bore almost no resemblance to the elegant gentleman who strolled the House of Lords.

"Belle might as well eat violets," she said. "Nanny Plum says that she doesn't care for vegetables and throws them to the floor."

Miles shrugged and stretched out beside her, his eyes expressing smoldering interest. "Have I told you recently how exquisite you are? Better than a violet."

"Now and then," Daisy said, dimpling.

"Are you certain you don't feel like impulsively inviting me to your bedchamber?" His smile made desire burn in her core.

Behind him, Belle rolled to her back, meditatively chewing more violets as she stared at shifting leaves high above them. Daisy wasn't an experienced mother yet, but she recognized the look of a baby contemplating a nap.

"Thank you for bringing me here," Daisy said, avoiding the question. "I feel as if we're lying on a flowery mattress."

Miles propped himself up on one elbow and cocked an eyebrow. "A purple mattress?"

"If only mattresses smelled like this," she said dreamily.

Miles sniffed loudly. "Green wood with a touch of mushroom."

Before she could answer, he rolled back to his other side to make sure that Belle was all right. Not surprisingly, Miles had shown himself a wonderful father: loving, protective, endlessly celebratory. Everything that Daisy's father had not been.

She loved her husband. She believed that he loved her. Deep in the night she couldn't stop herself from gloating over the evidence: the longing in Miles's voice, the ferocity in his eyes when he threatened to kill Frederick, the intensity with which he regarded her, praised her, kissed her, touched her.

"Our daughter is asleep," Miles said, gently picking up Belle and tucking her into her basket. He draped a piece of lace over the top to make sure that she wasn't bothered by an errant bee. "Belle has grown so much that she won't fit her basket soon."

"We'll keep it for her." They had already decided that when Belle was old enough, she would be told about the mother who had birthed her.

"Naptime," Daisy said, throwing an arm over her eyes, which didn't hide her smile. She loved the game they were playing. Courtship was delicious.

Sure enough, her husband placed a heavy thigh over her legs. A spark of excitement went through her body. "I'm not sleepy." Miles's voice lowered to an intimate burr. His left hand curled around her cheek and tipped her face toward him. "May I kiss you?"

"Yes," Daisy whispered.

"Just to be honest, I live in hope that you will impulsively beg me to do more than kiss you."

"Here? In the woods?" Daisy managed a semi-scandalized tone. She already knew that given rein, her husband planned to make love to her in the drawing room, the carriage, and several other unlikely settings.

"I've been thinking about horseback," Miles said musingly, his eyes glowing with desire. And love. And possessiveness.

Daisy pulled him down to meet her lips. "I do love you," she confessed, her heart overflowing with emotion that could not be corralled. "I always loved you, even when you left me naked on the bed. I couldn't stop myself."

Miles's eyes fired. "My only explanation is temporary insanity," he said, his mouth drifting over her cheek. "The moment I climbed into the carriage I knew I'd made the mistake of a lifetime."

"You are the only man I will ever love," Daisy said from the depths of her heart.

"I would die before I left you again," he told her. "You—you and Belle—are my life." His voice ached with emotion.

A large hand ran up her thigh. "Please beg me, Daisy." His tongue danced with hers until a raw male sound broke from his lips. His hand trailed up her leg to the top of her silk stocking, pausing to tease and seduce.

"Ma," Belle said drowsily.

Miles turned his head, reached over, and plucked up the lace fichu. "She's still asleep."

"You're such a wonderful father." Daisy couldn't help a smile so wide that her cheeks hurt. "Everything my father wasn't. Loving and protective."

"Our daughter is blessed to have you as a mother."

Miles levered himself away and rose to his knees. A ring sat on his palm.

"Will you marry me, Daisy?"

A shaft of light came through the leafy roof above them and caught a large jewel that danced with purple flecks.

"I love you. I have loved you for more than a year. I can think of no greater blessing than to be able to live with you and Belle, to be yours, to have children with you, to grow old with you." His eyes searched hers, dark with tenderness and love.

Daisy came to her knees, feeling drunk with happiness. "Yes." And then, as the hint of uncertainty disappeared from his eyes, "Yes, Miles. Always yes. It's always been you."

"I'm devilishly bad-tempered when I'm tired, but I swear that I will never knowingly hurt you. I will never walk out of the house in a rage."

He picked up her left hand and slid off her wedding ring, replacing it with a ring graced with an outrageously large diamond that was violet, with dusky purple depths. "I sent to London for a violet that will never wilt."

"Oh, Miles." Tears pricked Daisy's eyes as she reached up to kiss him. "I love this ring."

"Do I need to say something about how my love will never wilt? I'm not poetic. But *my love will never wilt*, Daisy. Never."

She believed him. Miles was on his knees, his heart and soul stripped bare. His face shone with love and desperate desire, the two so intertwined that they couldn't be separated.

Their molten, loving kisses made a joke of *begging*. Words were superfluous when two people can say so much without them. As fierce need sprang up between them, Daisy melted backward onto the blanket.

She took a deep breath. "Will you please share my bed tonight, Miles? Make love to me?"

His smile was blinding. "Make our vows legal? So that you're mine until death?"

Daisy nodded.

He picked up her left hand and slid her wedding ring back in place. "It would be my honor."

"I should tell you something first..." she said awkwardly.

Miles looked at her with his heart in his eyes. "I don't care what you tell me, Daisy though I might as well warn you that if you have another husband, I'll kill him and then marry you again."

A giggle burst from Daisy's lips. "I haven't!"

"Then?"

She forced the words out quickly. "Perhaps we might adopt my other half-siblings."

"Damn it, you scared the hell out of me," Miles groaned, pulling her closer. "Of course. I already have a Bow Street Runner working on it. The man will find them, and we'll bring them home."

"There may be several children," Daisy said, shamed again by her father's behavior.

Miles rubbed his nose against hers. "*Our* children. All of them."

"I'm particularly worried about the girl who's my age," she confessed. "My mother said she looked just like me."

"So beautiful as to be vulnerable," Miles said, nodding. "The Chelsea Orphanage is not a terrible place to grow up, Daisy. She may be working as a perfectly respectable lady's maid."

"My mother thought it was too much to ask you, that I would be taking advantage of you."

"Please take advantage of me," Miles said, grinning. His fingers sank into her thigh.

Daisy nipped his bottom lip, which led to a crushing kiss, his hand ever sliding ever higher. The ache between her legs tightened.

"How do I take advantage of you?" she whispered when his fingers were toying with the curl of hair between her legs. A cry caught in her throat. "Miles!"

"Just by allowing me to touch you." His voice was low and greedy. A broad finger slid into Daisy's slick warmth.

She gasped as heat swept up her legs. They were still kissing, but Daisy couldn't concentrate. Her hands curled around his biceps, but her attention was focused on the broad, callused finger that was gently, oh so gently, sending heat surging through her body.

"Miles," she gasped, tearing her mouth away from his. His caress was so soft that it was driving her mad.

"Tell me," he growled, eyes on hers.

The air seized in Daisy's lungs. She couldn't say—it was so unladylike—so ... "Harder," she whispered, her voice aching and desperate. "Oh, please, *please*, Miles." Her hips arched up against his hands.

He cursed in a low voice, and a second finger slid inside her, filling her. He moved down her body, pulling up her gown. She scarcely noticed, her toes curling, bliss just out of reach.

"This doesn't hurt?" he growled.

"No, no, no." Daisy arched her hips again, forcing his fingers deeper, wider.

With a male grunt of satisfaction, a third finger filled her. Miles nipped her thigh and before she could prop herself up to see what he was doing, his tongue lashed her core.

Sensual delight crashed over her head, tossing her into a deep sea. Miles made a purring noise as he explored her sensitive spots, while Daisy gasped and stifled her cries with an arm over her face until lightning abruptly streaked all the way to her toes. He coaxed her through wave after wave of pleasure until Daisy opened her eyes to find herself breathless, sweat coating the back of her knees, her legs scandalously askew.

Her husband was propped on one elbow beside her, smiling. His eyes were wild, and he was licking his fingers.

"May I take you home to bed?" he growled.

Daisy's mind felt as blank as a field in the grip of a winter storm. Her eyes moved slowly from the possessive hunger in her husband's eyes to the exquisite plane of his cheekbones to his lower lip.

"Daisy?"

She opened her lips to answer...

"Moo!"

Episode 117:
Your Loveable Parts

Miles, Daisy, and Belle walked back from the woods to find the manor house dreaming in the afternoon sun, the main rooms clean and quiet, their butler nowhere to be seen. When Miles poked his head into the nursery, Nanny Plum was sitting by the window, folding a stack of tiny garments.

"There she is!" Nanny cried, springing from her seat so quickly that clothing tumbled to the floor.

Belle hid her face against Miles's shoulder as if she were shy—which she was not—and then peeked at her nanny.

"Please come to me?"

With a radiant smile that suggested confident assurance that everyone in the world loved her, Belle held out her arms.

"Who's the best baby in the world?" Nanny crooned. "My little Bluebell, that's who ... "

The sound died away as Miles closed the door to the nursery.

When he slipped through the door to their bedchamber, latching it for good measure, Daisy was leaning back against the headboard, wearing a chemise.

Nothing but a chemise.

Miles stiffened, every muscle in his body clenching. The garment was translucent and embroidered with just enough scattered blossoms to draw a man's focus to the pale pink nipples visible between a sprinkle of rosebuds.

He peeled off his shirt and tossed it to the side.

"You did promise to show me your loveable parts," his wife said, looking appreciatively at his chest.

Miles tried to force some words from his throat, but all he could manage was a hoarse "Right."

He stripped off his boots, breeches, smalls...all the garments by which men hid themselves from the world, until he stood naked at the side of the bed: unfashionably burly, unbecomingly hairy, with an extremely large cock bobbing inelegantly against his belly.

Daisy looked him over slowly, a light in her eyes telling him that every part of him was lovable.

"I'm arrogant," he told her, making sure she knew what she was taking on. "Angry and disillusioned, because of the criminal behavior I witnessed and couldn't punish. I am ashamed of my rakish past. But I love you, Daisy. I love all of you, every part of you, mind, body, and spirit."

She came up on her knees, which meant that her chemise pulled against her generous breasts, the swell of her hips, the straw-colored curls between her legs, and held out her arms. Miles went to his wife, because he would always go to her.

She was his, and he was hers.

In the end, he ripped the chemise from her body so that he could lick her nipples and make love to every lovable part of her. It wasn't until she was shivering, whimpering, and pleading that he braced himself over her. "Ready?"

"God, yes," Daisy said. With feeling.

"There's no going back. You'll be mine, Belle will be mine, your horde of half-siblings will be mine, too. You'll become my family. Ask my sisters: I never give up on my family."

Her hand caressed his cheek. "I know. You will shout when you're tired, and walk the floor if one of us is teething, and love us unto death. Did I cover everything?"

Miles nodded.

"You'll be *mine*, as well," she reminded him.

"I can't imagine a better fate." He glanced down. "My cock is thicker than my fingers."

Daisy's lips curled up. "I'm looking forward to that." Her eyes promised a life he had never imagined: one of decency and love and desire.

His voice rasped from his heart. "You're going to kill me."

"Let the deflowering commence!" Her eyes were lit with pure anticipation.

"It may hurt," Miles said, hating that idea.

"So I've heard. But I'm already aching." No man could have refused that plea.

Daisy's reaction to the said deflowering was a shiver and then a request that Miles go faster. She wiggled, sending fire through his body. "Actually, could you come deeper?" Her voice was intoxicating, a mixture of desire and happiness as potent as any siren's song.

When Miles pushed up one of her legs and stroked into her, harder and faster, his wife's eyes widened, and a low moan broke from her throat. Her hands clamped on his shoulders. "I think I finally understand Byron's poetry."

The only poetry Miles wanted came in the form of Daisy's cries. The very fibers of his being were focused on making sure that his bride enjoyed herself. Found enjoyment. Fragments of thoughts flew through his head like cracked china. Daisy's moans. The way she arched her neck. The way her legs curled around his hips.

The whole of it. The profound joy of making love to his wife.

When he finally rolled onto his back, sweating and exhausted, he thought dimly that he was the luckiest man in the world. Daisy lay beside him, air sobbing from her lungs, but a minute or two later, she turned her head, and he saw a smile in her eyes.

She swung herself over him coming down on her knees, wearing only a violet diamond and a wedding band. Miles crossed his hands behind his head and enjoyed the fact that his body responded to her as if he were a mere lad again.

"I have an idea," Daisy announced. She wiggled her hips side to side, and he drew in a sharp breath. "It's something I read about. I couldn't envision it, but now I understand."

Miles's attention was caught by her breasts, because there they were in front of him, gloriously lush, reddened by his lips. "Did I bite you?" he asked, looking closely.

"You are marvelously obedient when I said 'harder,'" Daisy told him. She bent forward, bracing her hands on either side of his head. "I finally figured out what you meant," she said, easing down onto his cock with a blissful expression.

"What?" Miles grunted. It was all he could summon up.

"Some parts of you *are* more lovable than others," Daisy said, joy liquid in her voice.

Episode 118: Epilogue

One year later

"The outside fork is for salad," Daisy informed her oldest half-sister.

"Lettuce is for rabbits. If this is a dessert spoon, what do you use to eat rabbit stew?" Pandora wasn't Daisy's twin, but close enough: the same blue eyes and silvery hair, but with a more elegant nose and a distinctly inelegant manner of speech.

Which made sense since she'd grown up the beloved daughter of a carnival barker, albeit one whose tinctures were sold in the best stores throughout the kingdom. Miles had taken one look at Mr. Gale and pronounced him a swindler, but he had to admit that the man was a charming swindler, who adored his adopted daughter. For her part, Pandora was fiercely intelligent with a wry, firecracker wit that regularly had the household in fits of laughter.

Daisy glanced down at the shining place setting. Two silver forks to the left, two knives to the right, and a dessert spoon and fork above the plate. "We never serve rabbit stew at a formal meal," she explained. "Roast rabbit, perhaps. But not stew."

Pandora groaned. "The meal sounds as much fun as being deserted on an island. No beer. No rabbit stew. No rye bread?"

"Never."

"It's as if there's a conspiracy to ruin our figures," Pandora said indignantly, putting her hands on her hips.

Daisy frowned, since two months ago she'd reached the point in her pregnancy when she had no figure.

"Beer and rye bread!" Pandora said, plumping up her breasts before her hands went back to her hips. "Not to mention my arse. I have a fantastic arse." She took a hasty step back. "Are you about to hurl again?"

"Perhaps." Daisy put her hand on her huge belly and waited it out. Finally, she took a deep breath. "I thought I was done vomiting a few months ago. It doesn't feel fair to have started again this morning."

"My father makes a tincture of ginger root, like ginger beer," Pandora suggested. "It settles a woman's stomach."

On finding out that Mr. Gale sold "cures" for everything from hair loss to fevers, Miles had made Daisy swear never to swallow one of those potions under any circumstances. "I've been using your father's Essence of Pearl cream," Daisy said, dodging the subject.

Pandora frowned, looking vaguely alarmed. "We have lovely skin. You shouldn't muddle it with that rubbish."

"Your father gave it to me," Daisy protested.

"You're so naïve. I don't know how you ever survived to your twenties."

"You just told me to drink his ginger brew!"

"Some things are good, and others aren't," Pandora explained. "We sell the pearl cream under three different names. He gave you the one for ladies, but it's just a mixture of wheat bran and vinegar. Costs nothing and sells for a lot. Throw it out."

Belying Daisy's fear that her eldest half-sister might have been shunted into a life of crime or hard labor, Pandora had been adopted as an infant and raised by her doting, extremely rich parents. She had been happy to meet Daisy but expressed absolutely no wish to be introduced to polite society—until her father and mother begged her.

"Iffen it don't work out, you'll be home with us in a trice," Mr. Gale had pleaded. "Did I get where I am by saying no to opportunity? What have I taught you, girl?"

"I don't like pretending that my father's dead," Pandora said now, pushing one of the knives slightly to the right so that it was in perfect alignment with its fellow.

"Unfortunately, our father *is* dead," Daisy said. Lord Wharton had died two months after her wedding. Only his valet had cried during the funeral.

"My real father," Pandora said moodily. "I like being with you, but the rest of this foolishness? What's more, I don't want to get married."

Daisy eased into a seat, clutching her stomach as if that would stop it from turning upside down. "Why not?"

"Most men I've met are boring. Gentlemen don't seem much better, your husband excluded. In fact, they might be worse, because they're so spoiled."

"You merely need to find the right one," Daisy said. Something odd was happening; Under her fingers her stomach hardened and then seized up. As she glanced down, she discovered to her horror that she had peed all over the Aubusson carpet.

"Baby's coming," Pandora said cheerfully. "Luckily for Hobbs, me dad has a cleaning solution for that." She pulled Daisy upright. "Let's get you upstairs and call the midwife, shall we?"

Daisy made it to the dining room door before she stopped and gave a little scream. Her entire body clenched as a wave of blinding pain swept up her legs.

Miles burst out of his study, his eyes wild. "Is the baby coming?"

"Shoo," Pandora said, over her shoulder as she drew Daisy toward the stairs. "A birthing chamber is no place for men."

Miles paid her no attention, which allowed Daisy to collapse into his arms when another contraction wrenched her body.

"I thought they were supposed to be spaced apart!" Daisy wailed.

"Our hips are designed for this," Pandora observed. "You'll get through it in half the time compared to a girl who's got the waist of a greyhound."

Daisy clutched her sister's arm. "I'm so glad you're here."

Pandora leaned over and kissed her cheek. "So am I. Now *you*," she said to Miles, "Make yourself useful. Carry Daisy to the bedchamber."

Before they could move, another wave of pain hit. A moan escaped her lips, and Miles's arms tightened around her.

"Baby's going to be born in five minutes at this rate," Pandora remarked, turning to run up the stairs.

As soon as the contraction relaxed, Miles swept Daisy into his arms. "Bundle of laundry again," she muttered, leaning her sweaty forehead against Miles's chest.

By the time they reached the bedchamber—having stopped halfway when another contraction hit—a canvas cloth and a sheet protected the mattress. Pandora was drying her hands on a clean piece of toweling.

Miles set Daisy onto her feet.

"Wash your hands twice," Pandora ordered, pointing to a bar of soap, a basin, and a pail of water. "Daisy, you first. Everyone needs to be clean."

"Is that one of your father's concoctions?" Miles demanded. "It's gray. The soap is *gray*."

"Soda ash. They've started to use it while doing amputations to stop infections. Wash," Pandora said in a ferocious voice. "I only found my sister a month ago, and I won't have her dying of childbirth fever. Nor the babe, either."

Daisy stumbled to the basin and washed her hands, followed by Miles. The midwife put up an argument, but gave in when Pandora threatened to toss her out the window.

Master Josias Devin, named after his paternal grandfather, came into the world with a howl of rage. He briefly calmed when he was put in his mother's arms, but resumed his screaming when he was taken away from her. He missed his comfy, snug bedchamber; he didn't like sunlight; he *really* didn't like being bathed by his Auntie Pandora.

When a tall man cuddled him against his broad chest and congratulated him on having such a fine set of lungs, Josias settled from howling to crying.

But it wasn't until a little face ringed with silvery blonde curls gave him a poke and said, "No cwying!" that he realized that the world had more to offer than glaring light and discomfort.

He lay quiet in his quilted crib, blinking up as his sister kissed him on his cheek. "My baby," Belle said with satisfaction.

Daisy, lying back exhausted, managed a hazy smile.

They had located two siblings in addition to Pandora in the last year, both of whom had been happily adopted years ago, and neither of whom had any interest in joining polite society.

The Chelsea Orphanage had been brutally practical in their explanation: beautiful children were invariably adopted in the first month of their residence, just like the cutest puppies. One look at his wife's teary eyes led Miles to pledge more money than the orphanage had received since its founding—to be used to support the children left behind.

Belle had at least two more half-siblings living somewhere in England, so Miles had contracted more Bow Street Runners to look for them. The chances were fairly good that the children were growing up healthy and happy with couples who desperately wanted a child and couldn't have their own.

"See how Josias is turning his head?" Pandora said to Belle. "He's looking for milk. Clever little chap, isn't he?"

"Milk," Belle said, looking around for her favorite mug.

"He's too little to share yours," her father said, bringing the baby over to Daisy.

Pandora swung Belle up into her arms. "Let's go find your milk, shall we?"

Being a sensible lad, not to mention a future lord of the manor, Josias instantly realized that warm milk was nearly as good as having a big sister.

Miles sat down on the side of the bed and leaned in to kiss Daisy. He looked like a man shocked by the sweetness of his own life. "Thank you, darling," he said huskily.

Daisy smiled up at him. "Please lie down with us."

Now that Miles wasn't responsible for miscreants in the House of Lords, he laughed every day and smiled every hour. And now that Daisy knew in her bones how loved and treasured she was, she wasn't afraid of arguments.

They were easily reconciled in the bedchamber, if truth be told.

A half-hour later, Pandora stuck her head in the door. "Belle is feeling lonely." After Miles nodded, she dropped the little girl on the bed and went to sit in the rocking chair next to the fireplace.

If there was an argument for marriage—and Pandora still wasn't entirely convinced—it was here in this room. Her eyes rested thoughtfully on her brother-in-law's face. He had tucked Belle protectively under his left arm like a baby bird, while his right arm held Daisy and Josias close to his side. His expression was so tender that it almost made her heart ache.

Almost.

Made in the USA
Middletown, DE
24 September 2024

61418225R00113